WHITE RHINO AND THE TANQUERAY CREW

WHITE RHINO AND THE TANQUERAY CREW

A HARRI SONTOUR MYSTERY

Carl H. Harrison

ISBN-13: 9781518612244
ISBN-10: 1518612245
Library of Congress Control Number: 2015917190
CreateSpace Independent Publishing Platform
North Charleston, South Carolina

Other Books by the Author

A Tramp in England
A Tramp on the Line
A Garrulous Tramp

Dedication

For my other brothers

Forward

Much of the following is true, some not quite so, but it is all unbelievable.

CHAPTER 1

You could be dead tomorrow, so if not now, when? It was Friday September 13, a quarter to four in the afternoon and already an hour and a bit into what was sure to be a dreary flight. There was something up, nobody was quite sure what but it involved finding something lost long ago.

Harri had left home at 1:15p.m. and ten minutes later picked up the chief, aka, White Rhino. As usual Harri was a little short of readies and desperately needed to share a cab to James Armstrong Richardson International Airport. They were headed for a meeting in Hawaii that The Driver had arranged. The Oregon based sub-chief had located a hideout on the Big Island that would be invisible to prying eyes.

On the night previous, in a misguided attempt to keep things secret from the true brains of his own outfit White Rhino had considered checking in for the flight online. His cunning plan was to do so in the early morning hours while ostensibly heading for a whizz, a man his age made many stops in the middle of the night. Later in a quiet moment over a refreshing and calming glass of red wine he reconsidered it was likely best not to generate the boarding pass at home. While the printer was set up down the basement of his modest war-time residence it had been constructed by elves in the early 1990's and its dreadful clatter could wake the dead. Fortunately he was able to check-in quite easily and without incident once they arrived at the airport.

In Harri's case his personal circumstance necessitated keeping a low profile and that dictated an absence from the internet. He knew well that the prying eyes of a prying government could do him real mischief and unhappily Big Brother is everywhere. When he presented himself at the conveniently placed walkup check-in counter an Amazon in blue forced him bodily over to a standup machine. Being insistent on covering his tracks he was not inclined to give in easily and so would have none of it. A little sleight of hand ensured that his check-in could not be managed electronically. The infernal godless machine was unable to recognize neither passport, credit card nor the reams of computer generated confirmation papers. Harri won the little skirmish and thwarted The Man. The Amazon had no choice but to allow check-in by personal contact. Sirens were screaming and red lights were flashing as Harri smirked to himself.

Having both successfully navigated the check-in procedures the duo next needed to navigate the baggage handlers. This was also a problem as White Rhino had brought along a guitar case, the violin case was just not big enough. The plan had been to keep it to hand in case of need but the stacked blond Gestapo counter-agent insisted that it be checked right through to Kona. They'd be defenseless for nearly eighteen hours, cursing beneath his breath White Rhino had no choice but to agree. Having won the little dance the counter-agent smiled viciously as the lads reluctantly headed to the large item baggage station. Fortunately the guy in front of them was making a clamour around the safety of his golf clubs. The guitar case slipped onto the belt with nobody in authority checking too closely. They were momentarily pleased with themselves until a dozy baggage handler innocently dropped a clanger. All passengers would need to identify their stuff at US customs in Vancouver by way of some sort of video process. They were immediately alarmed, if anyone poked around the case on the Left Coast they would be goners.

Meanwhile during all the confusion Crazy Dave's moll silently slid up to them. Crazy Dave was temporarily a wanted man, his likeness had recently been captured on one of the City's photo law enforcement cameras and he felt it would be best to arrive incognito. Travelling under his nom de guerre, *Turkey Legs*, he'd made his way to the airport in the trunk of the moll's car having secreted himself into his own suitcase to ensure an unseen departure. The moll whispered conspiratorially to White Rhino that the case containing the great one had just slipped down the baggage chute. He of course had some sort of plan to emerge undetected and join them on the other side of the security station. In a further nod to their mutual security he'd arranged a seat a few rows back from the duo to avoid anyone putting two and two together. Or more rightly put, putting one and two together!

Heartened by this news White Rhino and Harri headed for the security gate where the whole thing could still fall apart if they weren't vigilant. White Rhino was an Austrian national who'd fled the fall of Vienna during the troubles of 68 with forged papers that suggested he was of Mexican parentage. Nowadays this usually resulted in his having trouble of some sort at any border crossing, plus he was always his own worst enemy. He'd once spent a fortnight in a Guatemalan slammer having been caught trying to smuggle some *"tools"* to Dakota Slim's Roatan hideaway. On that occasion the false papers had been so patently ludicrous that there was little chance they could have passed any scrutiny. He was posing as a successful property manager!

Harri had his own issues with border crossings that dated back to the Viet-Nam War protests. Whenever travelling outside the country he was always wary in case that legendary picture of Teacher and himself holding the infamous rock out front of the American

Embassy on Donald Street ever surfaced. It was well known that the incident had terrified the Greatest Country on Earth. The embassy had struggled on in fear for a decade before finally losing heart and shuttering the office for good. That said he was convinced they still wanted their pound of flesh.

You can imagine the tension. They bucked up though as both believed heartily in that old Arabic proverb, *luck is the just reward of the skilful.* Putting their fears behind them they marched right up to the security gate entrance and put their faith in the age old saw. They were to be rewarded as they entered the security area. Just ahead of them was a clutch of the UofW Westmen women's soccer team. They were all resplendent in tight fitting black track suits with white stripes running down their shapely gams, and most were blonds. The so called trained professionals manning the complex electronic security apparatus could see nothing else. Our heroes breezed right through without even having to so much as take off their shoes or unclamp their belts.

They would later learn that fourth man of their little group had called in a marker from his alma mater to create a diversion. Dakota Slim had spent decades undercover pretending to counsel the criminally insane in the wide open frontier village that was Edmonton. This government sponsored employment had provided him with a well-spring of people with unholy talents to call upon whenever he had need of a favour. Such was the type of man he was that when he had need of a favour they were always granted. He would be joining up with the caravan in Vancouver.

Dakota Slim had spent his entire life living and working in the dark and cold that passes for a climate in mid-central Western Canada. He had been successful in all his endeavours even down to getting a hold of what every Canadian lad desired, a farmer's daughter. But he had a problem and it had been a lifelong addiction. While he claimed it was only a two a day habit the sad reality was that he was a smoker and while he had on occasion manfully tried to kick it he'd never been able.

Compounding his problem was that decades ago the government of the land decided smoking was one of the greatest evils known to mankind. Notwithstanding tobacco tax revenues were beneficial in paying for partisan government advertising the powers that be felt they had to make examples of the addicts. It was mandated that those horribly afflicted could only indulge their habit in the great out of doors. The immediate result was unfortunates cowering late at night in doorways or behind garbage bins with the rest of society's' cast offs. Smokers became pariahs in their own land.

While he'd never been one to care what others thought Dakota Slim had reached the point where he could no longer stand indulging his weakness outside when it was thirty below zero. Now, it was true he had a tropical island hideaway where he could smoke to his heart's content but at the back of his mind there was the nagging thought that his modest habit might come back one day to bite him on the butt, pardon the pun. He just could not risk giving up universal health care. In a typically calculated response he and the farmer's daughter had recently relocated to what passes for the tropics in his home and native land. This allowed him to struggle on with his curse in some degree of comfort and at the same time manage the Tanqueray Crew's business in Lotus Land.

When White Rhino and Harri reached the other side of security a supremely sedate Crazy Dave was awaiting in the no-man's land between where you are from and where you are going. He had clearly slipped through without detection and while they were curious they knew that having always been a closed mouthed sort of hood there would be no way he'd pass on just exactly how it had been accomplished. All they could do was dip their heads and tug on their forelocks in recognition of his talents.

There was twenty minutes to boarding so wandering about incognito suddenly seemed prudent. Crazy Dave and Harri chose to walk up and down the line of shops. Crazy Dave had not risked leaving town since the new airport had been built so it was all new to him and he was gob smacked at the now prevalent vending machines offering up cell phones and iPads. White Rhino decided that once again looking the dumb tourist was his best disguise. He stepped right up to a Bank of Montreal kiosk when a comely brunette enticed him over with an offer for the best credit card in the land. The cagey bugger killed ten minutes with the subterfuge.

Once onboard the airplane White Rhino and Harri found themselves in row 5 with Crazy Dave watching their backs from the eleventh. The lady next to him would use the airsickness bag immediately after takeoff and although she was stunning, under the circumstance Crazy Dave chose not to turn on his legendary Estonian charm. Discounting that incident it was an uneventful flight through a clear blue sky. White Rhino being ever eager to improve his mind read from his personal collection of 1950's scientific magazines. Harri finished off a Travis McGee story and had just begun Conrad's Heart of Darkness when the captain announced their descent into Calgary. This immediately put the boys on edge as doors opening could potentially allow someone intent on mischief an opportunity. Out the corner of his eye Harri noticed White Rhino had his hand in his pocket and was moving something about furiously, strangely he seemed to have a sock on his hand. Had he carried some sort of weapon aboard after all?

As it was to be an hour stop all aboard got off to amble about the waiting area. While others had been seduced by the airline's fare our boys had not partaken in food or drink while in flight. Fastidious to a "T" none wished to risk exposing themselves to the unpleasantness of utilizing a toilet on an airplane. That said, now being in some need they rushed to the facilities in the departure lounge and couldn't help but notice some poor fellow noisily tossing his cookies therein. He did so with some vigour for quite some time and they all wondered if he might have been poisoned? It was noted as an amusing aberration and ended there. Sadly none of them ever gave much thought to anyone else's trouble and strife.

Once temporarily settled in the tastefully decorated Calgary Airport departure lounge's comfortable seating area Crazy Dave and Harri noticed White Rhino was about to blow a gasket. It seems a mechanic for the airline in Winnipeg had owed him a favour, lots of people owed White Rhino. The mechanic had been personally tasked to ensure nothing was amiss with the airplane. He had assured White Rhino that everything was perfect and it wasn't. On that first leg out Hari's fold down table hadn't, and it drove White Rhino to distraction. There would be big trouble for someone in a week or two. It would have happened right there and then if White Rhino had been able to contact his fixer back in Winnipeg. Fortunately White Rhino was unable, or unaware that he had to switch his cell phone from airplane mode.

Boarding for the Vancouver flight was eventually announced and as a security measure White Rhino and Crazy Dave acted like big shots. Harri dutifully trotted on when his seat row was called to scout out any danger while the other two waited till the very last second to re-board.

It was an easy one hour hop and the views of the Rockies captivated their attention, except for Crazy Dave who dozed off. White Rhino and Harri knew they needed to relax and rest but circumstances would only give snatches of relief. The flight attendants foisting off coffee and tea brewed somewhere over Lake Superior the previous morning didn't help matters. Adding insult to injury, as the Canadian airline industry does so well, passengers were offered a choice of two baby biscuits or a small sack of dried out starch purported to have pretzel DNA. The boys were hungry, but not that hungry. The two that were awake secretly hoped that upon arrival in Vancouver Dakota Slim could be located quickly so that a stop for sushi and green tea could be had. Those who have studied the eastern culture know well the revitalizing properties of airport food-court sushi. Plus Crazy Dave was a great believer in avoiding red meat whenever possible.

Dakota Slim being readily found was just wishful thinking. They each harboured real concerns with Dakota Slim having spent ten hours in the Vancouver Airport. You see he had a long history of losing focus when deprived of fresh air. It would have made sense to call him but Harri would not allow turning on a phone in case their whereabouts were tracked. Harri picked up most of his surveillance information from cop shows on television during long cold winters so he knew how these things worked. Primarily though the real reason for not calling was that they all had cash flow issues and roaming fees would be disastrous to their fiscal stability. They would just have to locate Dakota Slim the old fashioned way, leg work.

The plane landed without incident around half past five and the three travelers regrouped in the departure lounge to plot the search for their erstwhile compatriot. It was no real surprise that Dakota Slim was not waiting on them in the lounge. He had the uncanny ability to disappear into any crowd and blend into any situation. He also had the knack of being able to meet someone and convince them that they were old friends. Then spend hours in the company of total strangers and have the evening culminate in his dinner being paid for. This and the previous mentioned issue of losing focus when deprived of fresh air meant things didn't bode well. That said the Winnipeg crew truly hoped against hope that he would be standing outside the gate when the flight landed.

Where the hell was he? They wondered aloud if he had received the message that they'd changed their itinerary. A week or so back it transpired there hadn't been a need to pay a courtesy visit on the Nepalese consortium in Gas Town between flights. That little bit of bother had died down as quickly as it had arisen and tribute no longer being required they'd made a flight change to something less onerous for fellows of their vintage. They were sure they had mentioned it, but maybe not as they'd a lot on their minds over the past few days. After a quick management meeting they decided to spend a few more moments hanging about incase he showed.

The boys shot the breeze awhile recalling the past and the three charter members of the old crew who were unavailable to assist in the search. Dapper Dan was living a quiet life holed up in a multimillion dollar river bank complex being waited on hand and foot. The Mechanic had retired from active service to spend his days questioning how he ever got hooked up with those he now referred to as assholes. Teacher was off on some clandestine mission in Saudi Arabia trying to subvert the government by introducing bacon and reruns of Baywatch to the populace at large. He'd never quite given up on the social protest movement. The three were suddenly quiet at the recollections and one was seen to wipe his eye.

By then they had waited about as long as they'd dared and rose as one. To the casual observer the three travelers looked to be haphazardly wandering about with no firm plan. This of course was the case and they quickly devolved to the usual pattern when any three were together. Two would loudly discuss some trivial item ad-nauseam and the third would seemingly separate from them in response. The third would for all intents appear to be looking for blessed relief from an idiotic discussion that should have ended a quarter of an hour previous. Of course the one who split off was in fact guarding his two brothers. In this case Harri was the guard and as he scouted he was also sourcing a table for them to sit at to refresh themselves. White Rhino and Crazy Dave were successfully pretending they had no idea how to order food from the Serbian server at the Japanese take out restaurant. It was very well played; passersby thought they were nuts and possibly *partners*, if you know what I mean.

They all felt better after the modest repast, that and the quick hammering down of a restorative glass of beer. They would have had tea but it looked a funny green colour. Things were loosening up as it seemed they had gotten out of Winnipeg unnoticed.

The big problem still remained, where was Dakota Slim? Suddenly as one they had a collective thought; perhaps he was now at the departure gate. It seemed like a plan so off they sauntered trying hard though unsuccessfully to appear a group of unrelated travelers. Sure enough their quarry was found sitting in the departure lounge like some fat and happy Buddha. All decorum and secrecy was blown away as the four old comrades couldn't help themselves but have a raucous greeting. Many heads turned in the crowded lounge at the display. Harri, for one, was always suspicious of crowds and standing there amongst the multitudes he wondered who goes to Hawaii in September. He didn't notice the irony in his own thought process.

Dakota Slim had also brought a guitar case as carry-on. As with White Rhino, he felt his *instrument* was too large for the more traditional violin case. Over many years they'd both carried on the fiction that their respective *instruments* were larger than anyone else's. None believed it of course, but it made them happy, so where was the harm.

CHAPTER 2

Once they all settled on the comfortably uphol-stered plastic airport lounge seats Dakota Slim recounted that morning's left coast morality play. It had all begun innocently enough on his island retreat across the water from Vancouver. On the day the Winnipeg contingent was flying in Dakota Slim had booked a 7:45a.m. commuter flight and had every intention of checking in at 7:00 for the short hop to the other side where he would meet them all at the airport. As he headed out the door that morn-ing he was startled to see the Max lurking over a cof-fee with a grin on her face. Instantly unnerved he was unsure if the wise one knew something or was just expecting the inevitable. Something was surely up?

He arrived at the local two bit aerodrome with plenty of time, or so he thought. As with Harri, the self-serve machine didn't recognize him and he had an agonizing wait in line for an agent. Standing directly in front of him was an ancient Chinese woman and her two yapping dogs. The old doll was taking way too much time checking in. An obvious ruse was being staged; anyone who has frequented a Chinese restaurant knows Orientals prefer cats. Dakota Slim quickly realized an attempt was being made to hold him back and it was working. By the time he was in front of someone with authority the airplane had already left and there wasn't another for hours. He couldn't help but consider it was not his fault and that strange mysterious forces were in play.

He'd always been fast on his tiny, girl like feet and he now rushed outdoors and climbed into the only cab in sight. He awakened the slovenly driver by slamming the door, three times. He demanded that they immediately set off for the ferry at Tsawwassen, an otherworldly village on the outskirts of nowhere. In the local indigenous language the name roughly translates to "*where the fuck are we*". The cab arrived at the docks with only moments to spare. Happily the ferry ride was uneventful except for a slightly troubling 45 degree list to starboard that our traveler managed admirably after dispensing with the breakfast he had earlier shared with the Max. Once over the water and again on solid ground he discovered his pocket might have been picked for he seemed to have a shortage of cash. Surely he hadn't forgotten to put his substantial bank-roll in his pocket that morning? Feeling a hot searing panic starting to rise in his gullet for the third time that day he glanced around furtively for a stranger to befriend and pump for cash but saw no easy target. There was nothing for it but to continue on with the cheapest possible passage. He boarded the sky-train with the rest of the riff-raff and soon found himself in the bowels of the airport with the expectation of hours of not drawing attention to himself to look forward to.

Instinctively knowing that the best offense was a strong defense he found an unattended bench and feigned a four hour and a bit nap. Later he read and surfed the net on his new tablet that a new old friend had bought him. Always concerned about his circulation he would continually stretch his legs every half an hour with a walk down to a watering hole. Upon his last return to the departure lounge he was unfortunately recognized by an unsavoury character from Alberta days named Les who had a less than stellar reputation for keeping his mouth shut. Worse yet he had his wing woman Roxy with him. They claimed to be on their way to San Fran to cheer on the Kiwi entry in the America's Cup. He was suspicious, clearly the pair lacked imagination and the ability to think fast. It was then the Winnipeg contingent showed up and possibly saved someone getting seriously hurt, or worse.

Elsewhere and flying direct to Kona from Portland, Oregon The Driver had his own issues.

There was of course a story around his originally leaving The Peg. Thirty-five years past a minor legal imbroglio in the parking lot of a Norwegian themed drinking establishment located in the southwest of his hometown had turned his life upside down. The statutes of limitations have yet to run out so suffice it to say he ran like a thief in the night. He ended up in Davis California hiding at the university where one day the Santa Ana winds blew a Joyce into his life. She would be the first of the hundreds of the Joyce of his dreams that temporarily filled space while he was awaiting his one true love. Like all the others that would follow this one was momentarily happy in the blissful ignorance that she had no hope of lasting. Keeping a low profile The Driver soldiered on at the university for years. It was during this period of his life that he accidentally discovered a talent for feeding cattle life affirming products made of cedar. He would later settle down to run his part of the Tanqueray Crew's operation from Oregon. He fell in love with the weather there, especially the way it rained every single bloody day.

The day previous to his Canadian friends heading out he departed his Oregon stronghold by way of Portland's PDX at a quarter to eleven in the morning. The flight was an easy one and he spent a few hours snoozing and the next few eating and trying to read, but he was tense. He was keen to arrive and ensure that all was in readiness for the four from Canada. While they were a laid back group who seldom got angry harmony could only be counted on if everything was perfect. When they got angry it was not pretty. Crazy Dave was not known as *Turkey Legs* for nothing.

Thanks to time zone changes The Driver's flight made its scheduled stop in Honolulu around noon. Upon arrival he made the dash for the connection to Kona with something weighing on his mind. A day or so previous, Shady Norm, the disreputable owner of a disreputable dive shop, had offered to pick The Driver up and drive him up to the house on the hill. Shady Norm was looking for something from him and The Driver was not sure he wanted to give it. Not needing any aggravation before the arrival of the boys he desperately wanted to avoid any negotiations around anything with anybody, especially Shady Norm. He was worried that he'd have no choice though.

Before leaving the states he had put Shady Norm off with the weak excuse that he was unsure which of three connecting flights out of Honolulu he would be on. For years The Driver avoided pre-booking flights to make it difficult for anyone to follow his movements. He preferred to walk up to airline counters and purchase tickets when and as needed using small bills and handfuls of change which he liberated from vending machines at various Portland locations during twilight hours. He was confident that this admittedly cumbersome process kept the other side off balance and he used it this day to keep Shady Norm at bay.

Once landed on The Big Island he took a cab to the house and the short trip turned out to be rife with danger. The ride up to Holualoa was piloted by a fossilized Russian émigré. To pass the time and cajole for a larger tip, as all cabbies do, he'd muttered away in his almost undecipherable accent that he had once fallen big time for Sarah Palin after reading old articles in Newsweek Magazine and viewing some photo-shopped photos on the internet. When the old codger learned Sarah could see Russia from her kitchen window he had walked across the ice covered Bering Sea to make good his escape from the gulag where he had been imprisoned since the Stalin days. The questionable governor had inexplicably rejected his advances out of hand and to his credit he had quickly moved on. He managed to stow away on an Italian cruise ship that had docked in Anchorage. Then the fearless git had leapt over the side and swam ashore in Kona as it sailed by the island some months back. Needing work he followed the age old typically pattern of non English speaking new arrivals, he got a job driving a hack. Unhappily all those years in Siberia meant he had forgotten how to drive on anything but snow and ice. On the ride up the hill The Driver had real fears that the ancient Russian would not successfully navigate the tropical road.

Upon finally arriving at the house it was discovered to be in good condition with no obvious sign of any other intruders. There was evidence of bugs, but not the electronic kind. While still edgy from the drive up the hill he immediately found some readily available transport and drove back down to Costco for supplies. Crazy Dave would only eat Costco pickles.

Naturally, once at the check-out he discovered to his horror he'd left his wallet on the table back at the house so he had no alternative but to go back and fetch it. What else could he do? He then returned to Costco and supplies were purchased. Five dozen eggs, salads in bags, dinner rolls, milk, the biggest jar of Polski Ogorkis he could find and a gallon of gin. Dakota Slim needed to be kept well lubricated or he would snap and if that were to happen only God knew where things would end up.

He lamentably discovered too late that Costco had a philosophical problem with retailing tonic water so he made a mental note to pick up some elsewhere the next day. Doing without the tonic would obviously put the whole deal in jeopardy. Provisions on hand he had a quick and tasteless dinner and fell exhausted to sleep at 7:00p.m. local time.

He awoke with a start and a feeling of dread in the middle of the night and in a cold sweat remembered that weeks back he'd made a sort of commitment to Shady Norm. It happened that The Driver had some pseudo business arrangements on the island as part of his cover. He had done so by feigning interest in the purchase of an operation from the expat Canadian. Shady Norm wanted, nay, needed to get off the island in a hurry. That was why he'd been so keen to pick The Driver up at the airport. He couldn't risk The Driver being out of his sight while on the island in case his well documented flightiness shifted focus and fixated on some other deal.

Shady Norm shouldn't have been overly worried for somehow what had started as a disinterested ruse had turned into the real thing. Completely out of character and before he knew what was happening The Driver was having meetings. On the morning of the boys' arrival he awoke at 9:00a.m., an hour prior to a meeting with some quasi lower level government functionary, name of Nancy. He may have been late but there was nothing on earth that would induce him to miss his morning repast. After a quick cup of coffee and hearty bowl of colon cleansing porridge he raced down the hill to the meet at Honokohau Harbour in the casually borrowed pick-up he'd located unattended in a neighbouring driveway the evening previous.

The meeting with Nancy, her pretty boy assistant and Shady Norm was to supposedly review regulations relating to the Eel Cove dive site. They also intended to cover off the necessary permits involving the business Shady Norm was trying to unload. A business that records indicated regularly alternated between being underwater and then suddenly above. The Driver was pleased to note that Shady Norm seemed to get along with the government flunkies. Interestingly the following day White Rhino and Harri would spend a couple of carefree hours feeding the fishes over the side of a boat at the very Eel Cove they were then discussing.

Once the meeting was over he and Shady Norm had a quick coffee at the New Industrial Area to flesh out more details of the deal. It was then that the relentless and slightly desperate salesman let drop the operation actually consisted of a number of pieces that The Driver was unaware of, all of this six months in. When pressed for the wherefores and how comes it transpired that Shady Norm was part of a cult. Part of his entry requirements to the group was that all of his assets had needed to be signed over to the living god. Now he may have been a joiner but he wasn't a fool and he'd kept back some of his stuff from JW Cult Inc. He had cunningly hidden them by registering the assets in the names of a number of recently departed Hawaiians. Today in conversation with The Driver he confessed it was going to take some work to actually wrestle all the secreted vital components back from the dead.

The Driver had always had a terrific poker face. Actually it was quite beyond the norm and the Norm sitting across the two steaming cups of locally grown organic Kona coffees didn't realize this new information could be a deal breaker. It was possible there was still some semblance of a deal in the offing so The Driver wasn't about to throw it all away just yet. But he was wary that one side was more foot loose and fancy free with the facts than the other found comfortable. It was now a shaky deal and ever cagey he quickly decided it was best to sit back and bide his time. Sensing the wind change by the sudden reticence from his mark the relentless Shady Norm played the card he had up his sleeve. To oil the waters he suddenly offered a dive trip on the morrow out on the water for The Driver and his old friends. This piqued The Drivers interest and he nodded in the affirmative. As they were leaving the coffee shop Shady Norm said he'd get back to him in a couple of hours.

On returning to the house he had barely settled down to a tasty and utterly refreshing Kona ale while reposing on the couch when the phone rang. It was Shady Norm who told him there were spots available on the famous vessel Honu Iki the next day. The Driver was immediately wary; it was too soon and too fast. How was it possible that this was arranged so quickly and how could he double check all the security issues in time? He'd known Shady Norm had contacts but had been unsure just how powerful they were. He now had an inkling how powerful and he was seeing Shady Norm in a new light. He didn't like surprises, but then again good fortune shouldn't preclude taking advantage of an opportunity that fell at your feet. "What the hell" he said to himself, "sometimes you just have to take a chance".

Once that was settled it was time for some housekeeping. He wanted no aggravation from the freakishly cleanliness obsessed Canadians. Floors were mopped, carpets vacuumed and hot water tanks were turned on, but not all of them. He left one of them off as a cruel joke. A roll of the dice would determine who of the group would have freezing cold showers for the first couple of days and the thought gave him great pleasure. He had lived in the USA for decades but was still at heart a Canadian and knew well that Canadians are a respectful nation and totally uncomfortable when it comes to complaining. He knew that whoever drew the short straw would be unlikely to mention the lack of hot water for a couple of days. He was chuckling to himself as he swept the patio clear of the detritus of life before the trip into town to get the much needed tonic water. Boozing was in the cards. Little did he know the gin would run out the first day.

On the way down the hill he slapped the side of his head when he realized he could have saved some time by buying the tonic water on his way home after the meeting with Shady Norm that morning.

CHAPTER 3

MEanwhile, back in Vancouver Airport before boarding for the flight over the great blue sea each of the thrifty bunch purchased a large bottle with a built in handle of duty free Lamb's Navy Rum. The Driver had made it known to them a number of times over the previous weeks that the elixir was unavailable on the island at any price. Now, to a man they were dumb, but not so dumb as to miss such an obvious hint. It was well known in the circles they moved that The Driver had an affinity for the stuff; some of them had once or twice even worryingly suggested calling it a problem.

By 8:00p.m. they were well on their way and it was a lousy flight, not bug infested just uncomfortable. They had only just sat down when over the intercom the statuesque stewardess proudly stated that it was that airplane's inaugural flight. Perhaps none ever having sat or broken wind in the seats explained why they were as hard as mahogany. Further compounding discomfort was that the seat backs did not have the expected television screens. This was the result of a new airline strategy to generate further income by renting tablets to the captive audience for their viewing pleasure, for the modest sum of $10 a piece. Paltry though the sum might seem the cost wasn't within any of their budgets. It crossed through Crazy Dave's mind that perhaps the change to tablets had been made because there was no one left to cough up $4 for the earphones they'd been flogging on flights for years.

White Rhino and Harri were again seated side by side and had been inexplicably put beside one of the exit doors over the wings. In the event of an emergency the airline had unbelievably put responsibility for the safe egress of its paying passengers into their incapable hands. For over forty years the chosen two had been unable to agree on even the simplest course of action. With them in charge there would be little chance of success if any sort of tragic happenstance required that the door needed to be opened to help people escape. There was a final irritation adding to the pairs overall discomfort. The chair-backs in emergency rows did not tilt back. Apparently to do so risked the seat holder becoming too comfortable and so not attentive when and if required.

It had been said for years, or at least since the movie came out *that the force* was with Crazy Dave. Being always vigilant to collective safety he was again five rows back from the duo in the emergency row. He was momentarily wide awake but being awake was not really relevant for him to complete his duties. Crazy Dave had trained himself to register what his eyes saw during each rapid eye movement when reposed. He also had the remarkable ability that even when in deep REM sleep he was always aware of his surroundings. Although to be fair his fluttering eyelids gave views similar to what one experienced under the strobe and black lights of the Black Knight Lounge in days of yore.

The fourth traveler, Dakota Slim was well set up six rows back of their security chief. Ever the clever, conniving and cagey campaigner Dakota Slim had willfully arranged removal of the tenants of the two seats beside him. Since a child he had been able to engage gastric discomfort at a moment's notice. This talent meant he could keep a perimeter around himself free of anyone that might wish to do him harm. Once his row companions had relocated he stretched out across three seats and slept like a baby comfortable in the knowledge Crazy Dave was on guard.

In spite of all the precautions in place things were not as rosy aboard as they might have been. There were a number of couples with babes in arms cleverly positioned in rows opposite each of our heroes. The children were to screech uncontrollably the entire flight, and not in unison. Only one child was screaming at any given time. Crazy Dave swore he saw one parent, if in fact he was a parent; pinch a child that was momentarily quiet. There ensued five hours of an uninterrupted cacophony of bellowing children along with an assortment of subdued nautical curses from our boys.

There was also a surfer boy sitting beside Harri who would go on to read some sort of graphic novel on his tablet for the entire flight. The electronic screen of his infernal machine would light up Harri's personal space with its garishness. Where was a guitar case when you needed one? These aggravations couldn't be coincidence; somebody just had to have gotten to somebody. All of this guaranteed that there would be little rest for the intrepid travelers, with the possible exception of Dakota Slim.

Happily no one died on the flight though White Rhino's incessant gnawing on beef and pepperoni jerky did push Harri to the edge. White Rhino insisted it was for medicinal purposes and claimed it was good for his digestion. He also insisted that it negated the need for toothbrush or mouthwash, which assertion would be questioned many times in the coming days. If the flight had been an hour longer Harri would have snapped.

Immediately upon landing at Kona any hard feelings amongst the brothers that one of them had laid out on three seats while three of them had to sit upright immediately disappeared. It was nearly midnight as they exited the airplane and the warm night air was perfumed with the tropical plants and mystical fragrances of Hawaii. Palm trees were swaying in the trade winds beneath a blanket of stars and the four travelers were momentarily awed into incoherence, a state not too dissimilar from their natural one honestly. The airport building seemed to have no structure and they followed the crowd to the baggage carousel, the guitar cases being the priority.

An hour earlier, and a short distance away on that hot fragrant evening The Driver was preparing to motor down to the airport. Before leaving the house he'd used a cell phone he had recently found unattended at a baseball game to learn the incoming flight would arrive a few minutes early. His intentions were to park at the top of the small hill on the road leading into the airport. He hadn't the cash to pay for a parking meter having absentmindedly used all his change to pay for the flight from Honolulu. His cunning plan was to watch for the headlights of the airplane on final approach then simply roll down to the airport and park wherever he could. It worked out and the two mechanical transports arrived simultaneously. He loved it when a plan came together.

As the Crew entered the airport baggage retrieval area Harri glanced up and saw The Driver bounding over in what seemed like slow motion. A bear hug ensued which resulted in great quantities of Harri's straggly long hair being sucked down The Driver's windpipe, momentarily choking him. Now most fellows these days have short cropped heads, or shave them like billiard balls while some like Crazy Dave achieve the look naturally. Harri being ever the rebel and always reluctant to embrace the mainstream, felt there were so many with short hair it was his bounded duty to continue wearing his long in testament to the good old days. Besides, as he always responded when queried, *"why give up on a look that's worked so well for so long"*?

The bunch was all gathered about and pandemonium ensued when for the first time in nearly four decades all five brothers were together again. It was a moment in time that would never be forgotten and they playful punched each other's forearms to show affection as grown men are wont to do. Time passed and with his arm starting to ache The Driver snapped them all to attention. He suggested there was danger in hanging about so baggage was quickly grabbed and they headed for the exit. Ever the risk taker he had parked the borrowed truck in a no parking zone totally disregarding the danger inherent in such wild behavior. Impressive and admirable as that might have been, to be busted right off the bat would do nobody any good even if The Driver did have access to the best legal team in the islands. He had wisely prearranged the legendary predatory firm of *Shyster, Weiner, Screwem & Cox* to be on call with an eight day retainer.

They all raced to the curb as quickly and with as much dignity as their aged bodies allowed and the assorted collection of bags were thrown willy-nilly into the back of the white four-door Toyota pickup. They applauded the clever choice but when queried further The Driver would only allow that he'd found the vehicle momentarily unattended somewhere or other. Once they were all crowded within they discovered a surprise awaiting them. The Driver had originally considered a clever arrival welcome might have been to provide each of his four brothers with a traditional Hawaiian lei. That thought was soon put to rest as the cost would be $7 a toss, at this stage of their lives just how long could they last, two minutes tops? Truth be told he had experienced some hard times lately and was barely getting by on a much reduced fixed monthly income.

But he knew he had to do something as a token of his esteem for his fellows and it came to him in a flash of inspiration. In October of '76 The Driver and Crazy Dave had run into some temporary minor legal issues involving an underage floozy and they'd gone on the lamb to Oahu. While there Crazy Dave had developed an almost heroin like addiction to a crap beer called Primo. While preparing for this trip and in a rare moment of clarity he recalled he'd left a Primo can buried beneath a lime tree and on the Big Island as it happened. Never being one to either waste anything or spend a nickel if possible he'd immediately sent The Driver detailed instructions on how to retrieve the cache. The Driver, always having been one to do as instructed, did as instructed and while so doing chanced upon an eighty-five year old Guadalcanal marine veteran asleep in a wheelchair. The aged vet had magnificently wheeled himself up a hill to get a glance of a legendary prefab Vietnamese house that had been built on a slant; at least some felt it wasn't on the level. Once the old timer had pushed himself up the hill he was so exhausted he needed a little nap. Fortuitously the old codger happened to be sitting on a canvas sack containing four cans of beer. When The Driver came across the sleeping invalid he did what anyone would do who found themselves in such a situation. The beers were packed away in the truck and the issue around a welcome gift was solved.

Once everyone was in the truck the beer cans' tabs were ripped off like tough guys rip off band-aids. Unhappily, the second the cans touched lips in toast to a safe arrival a uniformed member of the local constabulary started walking up to a truck in a no parking zone. The Driver did what he always did and what he did so well, he got them the hell out of there before things could turn ugly.

Twenty minutes later they were at the place he'd arranged in the hills overlooking the sea and the city below. It was within a gated compound with a driveway that wound through an orchard of fruit trees. Fortunately the house couldn't be seen from the road and it all seemed quite secure for their purposes. Oddly The Driver was unaware of the electronic code for the imposing ironclad driveway gate and as was typical he didn't have any keys to the place either. When the boys would later leave for reconnoitering the pad was always left unlocked.

Once comfortably settled within the spacious digs the reason for the meeting was apparent, something was missing from their lives and had been for a long time. But what was it? Nobody could define it. Confusion reigned for a moment or two until almost on cue each of them dragged out a large bottle of Lamb's Navy Rum. The liquor was a testament to the strength of will they had each mustered for the search that was coming their way. The four soldiers were lined up on the kitchen counter and inexplicably The Driver handed each of them an opening salvo of gin. It was then nearing 1:00a.m. and it was wisely and collectively decided that one drink would be in order before calling it a night.

They talked of nothing, and they talked of everything. It was like they had been together the other day rather than the many decades that had passed. The expected rehashing of the glory years and the attempts at clarification of what had once been done, why and to who was begun immediately. The rewriting of the past would go on for days. By half past four a gallon of gin was gone helped along by a dozen pipes smoked out on the patio. Magically they'd somehow sorted out some modestly concise plans for the coming week.

The place The Driver had brought them to was a big rambling Hawaiian style ranch-house dwelling and as the evening progressed to daylight the group had thoughts of slumber. Unhappily over the many years that had passed all of the evening's attendees had developed a common affliction, a sonorous like rumbling from nasal regions when eyes were shut. These rumblings had become so loud and off putting to the general populations that to a man they were unable to comfortably sleep in a room with anyone else. Or rather, no one could comfortably sleep in the same room as any of them. Wisely The Driver had chosen a house with a room for each of them and over the early hours of the coming day he'd shown each their individual billet. It was a long difficult process as none could confidently stand, never mind walk.

Staggeringly and amazingly, while being so deep in his cups The Driver discovered a miscalculation, there was a bedroom short. Luckily being possessed of razor like cognitive reflexes uncommon in men his age he seized on an immediate solution. Harri, who seemed to be closest to nirvana at the time, was shown to the laundry room. In response to his plaintive pleading as to where the bed was The Driver laid out a couple of beach towels on the counter and graciously laid a few more on the floor, just in case they were needed to break a fall. The arrangement was acceptable to Harri in part because he had earlier decided on a night outside beneath the Southern Cross. The final arrangements would remain in a state of flux for a few hours more. Subsequently Harri located more acceptable accommodation on his own just down an ancient footpath of busted lava rock.

The sleeping arrangements being then reasonably sorted all returned poolside for one last great lashing of gin. When done with that final libation they individually staggered off to discover dreamland. The exception was Harri who stayed beneath the now dimming stars being quite unable to rise from his chaise lounge. At that point he still had every intention of remaining out of doors guarding his old friends from interlopers and ner-do-wells.

As the sun began poking its yellow head up off in the east the beautiful Hawaiian silence was suddenly broken by the roar of what sounded remarkably like a handful of chain saws coming from within the house. An hour later, Harri still on the patio heard a different type of noise in the bushes. While he was satisfied that it was not someone sneaking up to deliver the coup-d'-grace he suddenly recalled that he'd heard rumours of the wild feral chickens of Hawaii. It was said they occasionally carried off drunken Canadians whilst they slept. Knowing full well discretion was the better part of valour Harri crept noisily off the patio to find a spot to lay his head. His noggin was by then spinning round his shoulders in a clock wise rotation at the speed of sound.

CHAPTER 4

It could be accurately stated that morning came much too early for everyone. Then again it had already been early when they'd put their heads down. Three of them were up with faces in hands when The Driver started to prepare what would go on to be his regular breakfast presentation. A dozen eggs, onions, and tomatoes fired up together in an omelet. He was an expert at omelet making and when he was alone it was how he regularly broke his fast. In deference to the others he also whipped up ten waffles and provided an assortment of local fruits. Local meaning all picked five meters from the patio door. The breakfast menu would remain unchanged for the week. Dakota Slim being the cleverest of the assembled had determined how to best use the Mr. Coffee machine without flooding the kitchen, after only four attempts. He would later go on to cause a flood with a bottle of tonic water the details of which will be provided further along in this tale.

Harri was still trying to sleep in the separate residence far away from the others. Unhappily not far enough that their constant chatter and clanging about didn't raise a fire in his guts, he was in agony. Didn't they appreciate that like the guy in the washroom in Vancouver Airport he'd been poisoned. Of all assembled only Dakota Slim showed any concern about his well being. That concern was not unexpected as he and Harri had known each other since their first machinations with rules back in grade 3. They'd had their first friendly conversation while waiting in fear outside Mr. Klymkiw's principle office. There'd been an incident on the playground which resulted in a fat lip but the details of whose lip and whose fist was no longer relevant. Today, bless him, he'd ventured forth twice to try rousing his old friend from his death throes with little success. It was only with superhuman determination and admirable fortitude that Harri eventually dragged himself to the table, just as his mates were wiping dishes clean with fingers.

All being well sated they moved chairs back from the table to release the top buttons of their jeans, except for White Rhino who chose elasticized pants for meals to preclude that particular after dinner display. After sighing in unison during the unbuttoning they all complimented The Driver on his cooking excellence. It was to be only moments before someone questioned *"what about lunch"*? Fortunately a viable option for food stuffs presented itself out the kitchen window.

All well fed and adequately watered the five hardy souls wandered off into the surrounding jungle to gather food like their ancestors had done back in the mists of time. More accurately they skulked out like thieves to raid neighbouring gardens that were fortuitously hidden from sight by the thick tropical undergrowth of palm trees and tall flowering plants. When in the midst of the gathering Crazy Dave remarked that the bird of paradise with its lovely bouquet was as dead common as mosquitoes at a Winnipeg BBQ in July.

The lads went on to reap a bountiful harvest of limes, passion fruit, avocado, papaya, mangoes and a couple varieties of oranges. The diet over the coming week would prove to be the healthiest most had experienced in years not to mention the most cost effective. The limes were of particular value as they capably deadened the taste of gin, nobody seemed to be able to stomach gin without lime.

Your likely asking how was it that five aging gents could spend a full day flying halfway round the world, drain a gallon of gin and countless beers in a haze of blue smoke then go to bed as the sun was rising and still be standing that morning? Well of course the answer was they weren't still standing. The foraging had proven the final straw. They were all totally worn out so they'd laid down on chaise lounges The Driver had managed to rustle up from somewhere.

It was time for resting and they took the opportunity to rehash the debauchery of the previous evening. None of the five objected to acting their age for an hour or two while awaiting their collective wind to return. To be clear, that would be incoming wind and not the outgoing kind which White Rhino was then experiencing to the horror of his compatriots. This turbulence being the just reward of ingesting two pounds of suspect jerky on the airplane for its purely medicinal and dental hygienic purposes.

After an hour or so of relaxation made better by stimulating conversation the four from Canada showed the character of men they were. As mentioned, money was tight for all, but each had been truly troubled by recent news of a significant negative impact to The Driver's already meager monthly income stream. They didn't have much but they were resourceful and generous fellows. Not two weeks past at a football game of the league leading Winnipeg Blue Bombers they had quietly slipped away into a more pedestrian part of the new stadium. While 30,000 in attendance were enraptured by the theatrical cheerleading squad and the championship like quality of the team our kind hearted boys rustled thorough the home team's locker room. They purloined a number of t-shirts and jerseys boldly emblazoned with the name of The Driver's home town. Then at a risk even greater than the guitar case incident they'd cleverly smuggled the items to Hawaii in a plastic bag emblazoned LAUNDRY. That morning they gave their old friend the modest items in hope that there was still some wear left in them. The items may have been foul smelling but it was the thought that counted. There were tears of joy in everyone's eyes at the heartfelt acceptance of these modest gifts.

The scene was uncomfortable for all with everyone on the patio shuffling back and forth from one foot to the other with *"aw shucks"* seeming to be all anyone could get out. Something was needed to break the moment and luck once again interceded. The Gardener appeared on the scene like a genie from a bottle. Dwayne, so named by his mother, was a local giant among men when it came to providing the good stuff. He spent his days working on the local hospital grounds keeping the weed down (by which I mean the lawn kind) and the feral chickens at bay. Said flightless birds were everywhere on the island and the vicious beasts wandered with impunity. They would soon become a source of great annoyance to White Rhino, especially after Harri started referring to the one hanging about the house as his *little red-headed friend Helmut.* There will be more on these fowl things later.

In addition to the hospital gig The Gardiner also worked for a number of local residents who either were too lazy or too infirm to cut their own grass (by which I still mean the lawn kind). This life experience meant he'd become a keen observer of the human condition and knew exactly where the bodies were buried on that side of the Hawaiian hill. Over a smoke he recounted that the local dirt was so bad and pervasive that he had no alternative but to escape regularly from *the rock* to Las Vegas. He would often visit this holy land accompanied by his sainted mother to achieve some semblance of normality in his life.

A wee bag of a local herb was suddenly and graciously presented, surprising everyone. Purportedly, when taken to excess, it could greatly help with digestive issues that newcomers occasionally encountered with the local cuisine. It sounded more plausible than White Rhino's beef jerky and certainly more pleasant so he was thanked with profusion by all. Then, as mysteriously as he'd appeared he disappeared.

As some of the boys lazed about waiting for Godot plans were actually being finalized for the day's search. The Driver had already taken the bull by the horns when he took up Shady Norm's offer to arrange for a look on the high seas, and beneath. Knowing the inherent danger in the whole crew being aboard a boat four kilometers out on the blue Pacific he had wisely ensured innocent bystanders would be aboard the vessel as well. Then he went on to solve the problem of proper gear being required by strong arming Shady Norm into providing the needed stuff. If nothing else The Driver was a master of organization. In just under an hour all the Crew was ready for the long and winding road to the dive shop.

A little cutie on staff at the dive shop tried to explain to the aging lotharios that, yes, she did know better than all of them put together and, yes, what she suggested was exactly what they were going to need. She was a light hearted lass and as a gag had ensured that each of the Crew was provided a wetsuit two sizes too small for comfort. Knowing it was going to be a chore stuffing those bloated out of shape bodies into rubber suits and suddenly feeling remorse for her subterfuge she secretly recited a few *Hail Mary's* in penance and also in thanks that she would not have to witness the pending spectacle. While this was ongoing The Driver had slipped away to make a run to a well know Scottish restaurant to pick up some healthy eating choices covered in a tasty cheese like sauce. The Driver knew instinctively that to go out on the water immediately after eating less than nourishing food could prove dangerous, if not fatal.

The search began in earnest that afternoon.

Our five adventurers had capably disguised themselves to look like residents on a day outing from a nursing home. As the dockyard handlers were shipping the boat into the sparkling Pacific waters nobody would have guessed the tottering old fools trying to step onto the bobbing vessel without breaking a leg were, to a man, keenly trained and well developed individuals. To further the ruse it had been decided in advance that Harri would, as soon as possible, feign sea-sickness while presenting an image of false bravado by insisting to all and sundry that it was nothing more than exhaustion from the long flight and had nothing at all to do with a night of boozing. It was further agreed that Crazy Dave and White Rhino would follow his lead later during the three hour cruise. Dakota Slim reckoned that ridiculing his companions over the course of their discomfort would alleviate any suspicion that it was all an elaborate charade. This worked to greatest effect when Harri and White Rhino later took to feeding the fishes regurgitated Scottish fare.

The boat was a larger one with a captain they were told was late from commanding cruise ships in Caribbean and Alaskan waters. Today he was commanding a disreputable looking three person crew who looked like they'd been press ganged then keel hauled to reinforce discipline. In addition to the crew and our searchers there were a number of other passengers paying an outrageous fee for a promised idyllic adventure. There was a waif like Japanese lady of indeterminate years who had borne five children and had come to escape the obvious rigours of life on the coast of California. There were three tourists hailing from Omaha whose naturally inbred mid-western neurosis induced them to loudly proclaim to all within earshot that no visit to the islands was complete without a dive beneath the sea. They followed that by repeatedly stating they had more than enough resources to manage the eye-popping cost. Each of The Tanqueray Crew took this as a personal slight. Later they would be hard pressed to deny themselves some mischief beneath the waves involving a well placed knife against a rubber breathing hose.

It was the final couple our five would keep close eyes on. The male who towered over everyone had a bald head that from behind resembled a bullet. When he loudly and proudly announced he was a marine, or some such sort, the news went off like a rifle shot. Immediately suspicion arose in the breast of each of the Canadians wondering if they'd been made. His wife, or so she was introduced, was a stunning blond who carried her flotation devices with pride and honour. They were barely being held in check by a green bikini whose seams appeared to be on the point of failure. Whenever she was to struggle getting in or out of her wet-suit all eyes were on her along with unsolicited and heartfelt offers of assistance in helping to apply a thin layer of lotion between her and the rubber of the suit. Our five had difficulty agreeing who would keep an eye on the soldier and who the wife.

Much like the Royal family the boys had spent a lifetime selflessly separating themselves so they weren't all exposed to danger at the same time. Sometime it was simply ensuring that only two were ever in the same room, other times it involved being on separate sides of the continent. Today there were the unusual limitations of being out on a boat kilometers from dry land. The best plan they could come up with was for The Driver, Dakota Slim and White Rhino to scuba-dive while Crazy Dave and Harri snorkeled on the surface, a first for Harri.

It was a blissful cruise out to the dive site with much gaiety and laughter aboard. Once they'd arrived everyone immediately suited up and went over the side for the forty-five minute exploration of the sights beneath the waves. It was a wonderful experience and vice like grips on individual realities were momentarily relaxed. The water was clear as a bath before one immerses oneself and the great variety of sea life carried on what they were doing oblivious to the watchful and impressed gaze of land dwellers temporarily out of their natural element. The time in the water passed very quickly.

Upon his return to the boat Harri set about his predetermined role of not feeling well and noisily moved to the starboard side of the craft. His desire was to paint a realistic picture for anyone onboard or for those watching from any of the other dozen boats moored close by that he was damn near incapacitated. At the surreptitious rise of an eyebrow Crazy Dave also began to show odd symptoms. Meanwhile, White Rhino had surfaced from the deep without his underwater camera. He feigned great indignation and anger at the loss but later he and Dakota Slim were overhead discussing an interesting little insurance scam involving said camera. All the activity had the desired effect as no one onboard was taking the least bit of notice.

To reinforce the little drama being played out White Rhino and Dakota Slim stepped over to Harri who was quite convincingly languishing on his side in close proximity to the waves. The duo soon was laughing out loud at his discomfort solely for the benefit of any onlookers. Suddenly White Rhino joined in the pretending to be sea-sick pantomime and with great professionalism went beyond the pale by actually willing himself to turn green. A shade of green remarkably similar to the green of the previously mentioned well stuffed bikini.

Just because they were putting on a show didn't mean they'd let their guard down. Since coming back up into the air the lads had been keeping a wary eye on a helicopter off the port bow. There was a large yellow bucket like contraption suspended beneath it swinging wildly from a cable and the aircraft made repeated passes to and from the area the boat was anchored. The captain cavalierly offered that it was merely a training exercise for forest firefighting crews. The boys were of course skeptical and being attuned to this he desperately tried to change the channel by offering up an old urban myth. He told a tale of how years ago a devastating forest fire had been extinguished in the Californian northwest and afterwards a dead scuba diver in full gear had been discovered high in a tree eighty kilometers from any water source. The collective wisdom had it that the hapless diver had been scooped up out of the water by a similar bucket under a similar helicopter and then transported half an hour inland before being dropped from one thousand meters to his doom. An interesting tale perhaps but it did not divert the boys' attention an iota.

The Captain then tried to divert attention on deck by offering up a modest feast of Safeway's pre-cut oranges and fresh vegetables ostensibly to help restore constitutions for the second coming dive. This should not be confused with the other *second coming*. This dive would take place after sunset and required divers to sit on the bottom of the ocean with powerful flashlights trained upward. The light beams attracted plankton in great quantities and the plankton attracted great numbers of manta rays. These fighter jets of the deep would swoop into the light beams and open their mighty yaws to ingest great clouds of the delicious plankton. Some of these undersea flying beasts were five meters across and one of them would brush right up against The Driver and Dakota Slim. Lesser men would have messed themselves when sea monsters came amongst them but not those two. They were well known for nerves of steel

Never being particularly quick on the uptake Dakota Slim only realized once beneath the waves for the second time that it was his first night dive. It proved very challenging for him to sit on the ocean floor with a few dozen others holding flashlights as creatures from science fiction cruised overhead. His dive mask cut off some of his peripheral vision so the monsters would just startlingly pop into the light beams and it took strong intestinal fortitude not to panic. Interestingly up to that point in time he was utterly unaware that he was allergic to manta rays.

The sudden realization that he was so afflicted presented itself quite without warning. He sneezed twice and in so doing fogged up his mask. Unfortunately it was not just condensation that immediately covered the inside of his mask. This didn't help his experience much and his problems compounded when the rock he was perched on conducted a prostate exam. His heretofore strong intestinal fortitude began to give way and panic began rising like bile in your guts after a spicy Mexican taco.

Fortunate for all those down on the bottom of the sea the dive master was watching over them like a mother hen. Ostensibly his role was to monitor the divers' condition and their life giving air supply. The bile climbing ever higher meant Dakota Slim was looking for any excuse that trouble was brewing. Uncomfortable as he momentarily was he convinced himself that the security of his friends was paramount. He may not have been as security aware as Crazy Dave but he did his best and always tried to keep his legendary eagle eye out for two legged dangers. He quickly decided his group would be best served with him on the surface. Despite the risk of looking like a girly man he signaled the dive master he'd had enough and needed an escort back to the surface of the bounding main.

The two of them started up together but at seven meters beneath the stern of the craft he was suddenly left alone. Was it a trap? He swam slowly upwards remaining fully aware of the sharp propellers awaiting his noggin if he screwed up, or if someone lurking out of sight suddenly appeared and drove his head into them. Remember, it was dark except for his flashlight's eerie pencil thin beam only illuminating outward two meters. While scrutinizing the blackness of the Hawaiian seas for danger he was cognizant of a need to not forget to let air out of his BCD (buoyancy compensator for those not in the know). To forget that simple task risked a pop to the surface like a cork. He had never really paid attention during Mr. Andrusiak's high-school science class but at that moment he seemed to recall something about unrestricted expanding air proving problematic for scuba divers.

Up on the surface the wily group had earlier counseled Harri not to take part in another wetting; there were things that needed to be clarified. The excuse he was exhausted and not sea-sick was deliberately conjured to explain away his staying aboard during the second dive. This excuse was important as they had learned that a sea-sick person recovers if he floats on the water's surface. Harri's not going into the water for the cure would therefore be deemed suspicious. Besides, Harri's ego felt exhaustion was a more manly cover than a sick belly.

The boys felt some troubling information about the captain needed in-depth investigating. They already knew he had previously captained cruise ships in the Caribbean and Alaskan waters but on the trip out to the dive spot they'd also learned some troubling facts. Like that he owned a condo in San Diego and a fifty foot ketch moored in Fiji which he used to sail around the world. Something seemed clearly wrong with the picture. Why would such a well off individual be captaining a small dive boat for punters? Earlier Harri had casually pressed the point and the captain claimed it was nothing more than a year long vacation and his taking the present post was nothing more than keeping his hand in. Obviously there was more to this guy than met the eye. It was left to Harri to find out what the true story was while the others were cavorting on the sea bottom.

Through clever banter and a probing questioning technique learned during a thirty-one year tenure with a mysterious international banking conglomerate the so-called truth was discovered. The captain confessed that after a day of taking tourists out on the high seas he would sneak back out on the water with his employer's boat nightly at 11:00p.m. He would head ten kilometers out into the open ocean to a spot a thousand fathoms deep (that's eighteen hundred meters to those unaware of nautical speak) with a small trusted group. They would then dive down twenty or so meters and watch sea creatures rising up from the depths. Clearly this was crap and nothing but another cover story. He had obviously found Long John Silver's treasure. Unfortunately the boys had more pressing buttons to push and would be unable to take advantage of the knowledge on this trip.

Harri was still ruminating on what he'd discovered when Dakota Slim suddenly popped to the surface followed shortly thereafter by everyone else. Apparently seeing Dakota Slim heading upward had signaled the end of the evening's underwater excitement. Isn't that always the way, everybody wants to call it a day but nobody wants to be first. Once everyone was aboard hot chocolate was passed around like it was a tobogganing evening in the icy cold of a Winnipeg February.

Actually not everyone came back. An annoying underwater photographer seemed to have been misplaced. Troubling perhaps but it was thought by the less than sympathetic crew she was in good enough condition to swim back to shore. The crew made the boat ready as the Captain fired up the twin Chrysler engines for the thirty minute return to the boat yard. It was dark and the sea was somewhat choppy so Crazy Dave kept up his pretense of sea-sickness until safely docked.

It had been a spectacular trip out on the water and the boys were all truly thankful for the opportunity. But they hadn't found what they thought they might.

Upon return to dry land the truck was quickly loaded for the return to the house on the hill for thirst quenching and mind expanding nourishment. Once comfortably settled the boys took the opportunity to lounge alongside the pool and one or two actually went into what was considered in Hawaii to be frigid waters. Later a couple of them would spend hours trying to figure out how to turn the hot tub heat on. While it was a lovely house, being new to everyone little things like turning on the hot tub or how to change a light bulb, or even where supplies of toilet rolls were kept were complete mysteries. Things might have been different if the owner of the place had been in attendance but that would have created problems of a different sort.

Those not engaged in re-engineering the electrical system sat back looking up at the stars as the moon rose. Being easily awed, Harri noticed with awe that the sky looked somewhat different from back home. Caught off guard by this The Driver quickly changed the subject and pointing in some indeterminate direction mentioned that if one were to only swim four thousand kilometers one would reach Tahiti. At the time it seemed a reasonable plan to half the bunch for the following morning.

So, the evening's stage was set, a couple of them wasting time with electrical issues that were beyond their capabilities and a number numbed out on the patio. Focus was needed to be recharged. Clever man that he was Dakota Slim had anticipated this eventuality. He'd known there would be lots of time during the search for them to party and lose sight of the goal. He also knew on a spiritual level his compatriots would be lost without humour. He was a betting man and he bet that humour would focus their addled minds.

But there was a problem. He'd never been known to have any sense of what was funny nor even what was appropriate but he'd steeled himself to learn. Even lacking the basic knowledge of the medium he had charged himself with the task of entertaining them with a collection of jokes that would have the most impact on his bent friends. Unhappily his lack of any artistic talent meant his only real option was to steal jokes from any source possible. Being a proud man and not wishing to be accused of plagiarism he located an obscure volume of hilarity that none could possibly have read. A South African publication from the 1960's entitled *I Just Want out of Here - The Humour of Apartheid* by Nelson Boom-Boom Mandela.

Over the week the world turned as it would and while there was the occasional flop, not unrelated to the telling, he did hit many out of the park. All in all it proved worth his risk and it must be said that most of the jokes were wisely directed to the strictly male audience. He occasionally crossed a few boundaries but his telling of tales was welcomed, most of the time. Fortunately and as everyone already knew Crazy Dave was the one amongst them with the real sense of humour. He was always ready with bluster and eloquence to step quickly into any breach and relate a humorous tale if one of Dakota Slim's purloined jokes fell flat. Crinkling his jowls into a half-smile half-smirk and squinting up his blood shot eyes he'd look over his glasses and lay something hilariously funny on them. Occasionally it would turn out to be a huge groaner that would have caused Howie the Turtle to have actually turtled over onto his back. But it always got the same reaction, a room full of laughs. Undoubtedly the near constant partaking of the local herb enhanced his cognitive attributes as well as aiding with his digestion.

As night wore on the gin flowed like water over Victoria Falls, and smoke wafted above like cirrus cumulous clouds on a hot summer day. The boys all got pissed and not just pissed in the normal sense, they got absolutely legless. Unbelievably even more legless than they'd been the night before, or was that the morning before. Nonsensical arguments over nothing and discussions around things that could never be solved were loudly undertaken at various times over the course of the night. Each discussion would dissolve away as quickly as a teaspoon of sugar in a cup of tea with nothing ever resolved. To a man they were drunk, happy and exhausted and one by one they wandered off unsteadily in the early light of the coming day.

Strangely, the further away from sober the clearer what they were searching for began to come into view. Parts of the prize were beginning to form in each of their consciousness. It would just need a trigger for it all to come together.

All but White Rhino would arise the next morning with clearer heads than expected, or deserved.

CHAPTER 5

The island hideaway suited their needs perfectly. It was three hundred meters up a hill and provided a glorious outlook over city below and sea beyond. The weather was a constant; sunny first thing then clouding over by late morning with a possibility of rain in the afternoon, then clearing skies by 10:00p.m. It was very temperate and not at all like the blistering heat down by the shore. This suited the boys to a T as they all needed the comfort that constancy brought, though they would have all loudly disavowed such a suggestion if it had been raised.

The windows in the entire house were always open. Being the floor to ceiling variety allowed the warm tropical breezes to constantly and gently waft throughout the place. There was no need of heating or air conditioning systems here and this was unfathomable to the travelers from the distant land. The well known and familiar hum, drone and rattling of artificially heated or cooled air tumbling down sheet metal ducts controlled by some sort of thermostatically electronic brain had been very comforting to each of them since childhood. That familiar noise pulsing every seven and a half minute was now replaced by a distant but constant cock-a-doodle-do of feral chickens, which was not comforting to anyone. One inclined to conspiracy theories might have considered the regular seven and a half minutes crowing cycle too much like clockwork.

That morning, as usual, the boys relied on Crazy Dave to look after their security. He had been up since 6:00a.m. wandering the jungle with an eye out for any evidence of intruders. Utilizing his amazing telephone Crazy Dave took numerous photos and short films of the grounds which he would later intently study for any subtle changes in foliage placement. He diligently looked for any suggestion the opposition had found them and perhaps effected booby traps. All he'd found were feral chickens who spent their days crisscrossing the grounds calling constantly to themselves. It crossed his mind that White Rhino might well have been on to something the previous evening. While in his cups he'd suggested that the wild beasts may have been trained to monitor or worse yet, attack. Crazy Dave expected he'd have many a sleepless night keeping track of the wee beasties.

The suggestion that the chickens may have been tracking them was not so farfetched. There were regular sightings of the fowl things whenever the boys were out and about. Adding to the problem was that the flightless avians were too easily camouflaged and frankly when you'd seen one you'd seen them all.

There were of course other security issues. The Driver had always been laid back to the point of near unconsciousness and so responded to a request of possibly locking up the house when they were asleep with a firm no. He insisted that ensuring fifteen sliding doors were properly secured was too much like work. There was a weird sort of benefit to his intransigence on the subject; having the ability to escape danger by running outside from anywhere in the house without having to stop to unlock a door could prove handy.

While arguably being quite laid back The Driver was no fool and he had something else up his sleeve when it came to their well-being. He had commandeered the smallest room in the establishment for himself and had wisely ensconced Crazy Dave in the largest and best room. It may seem that would then make Crazy Dave the target in the event of interlopers, and that would be true. They all knew he was the best in that sort of situation and nobody had ever gotten the jump on Crazy Dave. For you see he slept little and when he did it was with one eye open. He was also never one to waste a moment of his time. He'd spend the long nights when others slept listening to the CBC or rereading the collected works of that Mexican philosopher, Carlos Castaneda. Those classical tomes had recently initiated an in-depth study of the therapeutic benefits that a hit of peyote might have in helping one occasionally fall more fully asleep.

Unfortunately White Rhino had chosen to go off on his own security detail that morning. To his credit he really tried to be ever alert, even when hung-over, but it was his lot in life to get preoccupied fairly easily. Breakfast time was calling and his absence being noted the rest had gone looking for their friend. They found him mindlessly scrubbing his feet beneath a swaying palm. He announced he'd found a bug in one of the rooms, but it turned out to be a four inch gecko.

That morning's presentation of yet another dozen egg omelet complimented with ten waffles plus the fresh fruit absentmindedly picked up off the jungle floor on regular forays was delicious. The food was again washed down with buckets of coffee that Dakota Slim kept percolating, or was that dripping. Over the meal they animatedly discussed the previous day's successful public pantomime of a gaggle of sixty year olds on holiday, though it had been somewhat hard to maintain. Without doubt the stellar dive boat performance of stomach churning turmoil by Harri, Crazy Dave and White Rhino pretending to lose control of their guts and colons had been masterful. It turned out to be so masterful that The Driver had already decided there would be more of the same the following day.

It was to be more tourist type stuff, deep sea fishing, and he'd decided that a couple of them should be off the hook (fishing analogy intentional) for a similar performance whilst fishing. It was determined that since The Driver was needed to man the transportation it would be unseemly if he appeared afflicted. They elected Dakota Slim and White Rhino to act the tourist when next at sea and they were fully expected to put on an Oscar worthy performance. It was also quickly and unanimously decided to avoid the Scottish restaurant before embarking on the fishing charter.

Everyone pitched in for the cleanup after breakfast. Unhappily any of their mothers would have dropped dead in shame at what the group considered a cleaned coffee cup never mind an acceptably washed frying pan or fork. Five hearts were in the right place though and it took very little time to complete the task. It really should have taken longer but there you are.

Once the domestic chores were dealt with they finally took the time to truly discover the place The Driver had brought them to. The jungle, previously beaten back from the house provided clear views in all directions and there were no neighbours within screaming distance. Majestic royal palm trees, presented like soldiers guarding a palace swayed in the ever present gentle breeze just along the footprint of the house. The three hundred and twenty-five square meter residence was built in the Hawaiian style and for those that know what that is, well good for you, for those don't, tough. It was plonked right in the centre of a hectare of grounds with a pool, a surrounding patio and a hot tub. The view stretched off to the horizon. It was said the place had been built thirty years back by a New York mob gynecologist whose time on the island had come to an untimely end when he'd conducted one too many internal examinations on a mobster's lovely.

On that first full perimeter reconnoiter it was discovered that the avocado tree outside an ohana, which Harri had commandeered for sleeping, had split under the weight of its load of fruit. Questions were naturally raised as why The Gardiner had let this come about. To which The Driver offered that avocados are not ripe till they fall from the tree. Naturally that information immediately gave rise to a boisterous chorus on the lack of quality fruit on the tables in their home and native land. They quickly agreed this was due to fruit being picked long before achieving optimum ripeness which led to tomatoes and bananas having that delightful woody taste and texture.

The five old comrades were all well pleased to be together once again. They had each become successful in their own right and had contented lives with much to be thankful for. They were all strong willed individuals and in the parlance of the Coca Cola pop-psychology they'd grown up with, each would have been labeled a Type A personality. They all held firm opinions on each and every matter and those individual opinions could not be shaken without the hand of God being involved. Yet after a few short days together there was a communion of sorts, a democracy of values, no one was the leader and no one was a follower and everything that needed to be done was got done. It was a wonder to see.

Now while they were all great friends and had all parked their egos it didn't mean they didn't know which buttons to push. Over the course of the week some buttons would be pushed as a group against one, or individually one on one. Each of them would receive his fair share of abuse and it helped keep an edge to the proceedings. Harri thought to himself that these were the best bunch of friends a guy could ever hope to have and thankfully they had been his friends every day for much of his life. The Driver would later wax nostalgic that the stars must have been aligned for all this to have come to pass. It was magic, and the magic was only broken by the call of yet another feral chicken.

Before heading off on the search in Kona, with the bonus of seeing some sights while pretending to do the tourist thing the group wandered off to pick even more fresh fruit. This time the bounty included passion fruits which Harri had never before eaten and he found them to be delightfully delicious. A bucket full of limes, oranges and the aforementioned avocados were also harvested. It all went reasonably successfully but they were unsure if White Rhino was still out of it or had misunderstood the mission. All he contributed to the hunting and gathering was a handful of birds of paradise. To be fair he was not used to eating less than a kilo of meat a day and possibly a lack of burnt protein induced a delirium which caused him to consider that the bird of paradise was in fact fowl.

Then they were off to Kona which was thirteen kilometers away. The road downhill was a back and forth black weaving ribbon. White Rhino continuing to feel the ill effects of what may have been too much drink or a bit of undigested cheese from the evening before began to complain vociferously that they were travelling much too fast for safety. This only induced the rest to implore the Driver to go faster which he obligingly did. Once in town he parked the truck where he damn well pleased and they walked off into the shopping mecca that was Kona. There were dozens of small stores along the roadway beside the sea and there were street vendors in abundance. Things were looking good for the tourist type stuff.

It was the case that White Rhino was the only one of the five with any real disposable income at this particular point in time, such as it was. Historically when flush he'd tend to flaunt it unmercifully and today was to be no exception. In a smallish shop managed by a grizzled one armed old fart he purchased a *genuine Hawaiian ukulele, handmade in Malaysia.* This beauty was not to be confused with The Driver's own exotic Malaysian beauty which was something else again. Obviously the shop keeper was unable to adequately demonstrate how to play the instrument or even the tuning technique but White Rhino would not be deterred. He forked over the 900 clams the one armed bandit demanded.

Our boys continued to wander about the crowded roadway in the beautiful sunshine and came across an outdoor stand manned by a stout Hawaiian artiste. She was offering up CD's of her self-recorded ukulele accompaniment to lustily belted out Hawaiian songs. Crazy Dave had always been a sucker for a woman of substance, or as some would say, of a certain girth and he quickly purchased two of her CD's. Obviously he used the opportunity to give her the once over and a smattering of his Estonian charm.

That accomplished they decided it was time for lunch and yet another restorative glass of beer. They found an establishment overlooking the bay that didn't seem overly busy for the time of day and chose a table against an outside wall to make sure no one could sneak up on them. They liked to have their backs to the wall; they were used to having their backs to the wall. Moments later the waitress appeared out of nowhere and startled them. To be fair their attention had been drawn to the sea, where fish were fishing, subs were subbing and sailboats were sailing. On a point of land off in the distance a red helicopter was landing at the sprawling spread of one of the founders of some computer company or other. It seemed a very busy body of water.

After a fine meal and a couple of craft beers it was time for a little shopping. Supplies were running low and by that you may read gin. White Rhino and Dakota

Slim had also got it into their heads that plumbing supplies were desperately needed. Locating a shop offering a variety of pipes was required and admirably The Driver knew just the place. Ten minutes later the five were in an establishment that catered to those with a keen interest in pipes that fired up well with regular use. After some thirty minutes of reviewing quality products White Rhino and Dakota Slim each found something that they mutually felt suited their individual piping needs. Then it was onward for groceries, beer and the good stuff before heading back up the hill for a lasagna dinner.

It would prove to be another full evening of remembrances, boozing and determining how to best plumb pipes for best effect. By over utilizing a combination of a new pipe and one of more traditional design Crazy Dave and Dakota Slim saw through the haze and figured out how to circumvent the homeowner's security system. It was discovered that the system had prevented easy use of the hot tub control panel, or so it was presented to the rest. Privately most considered it was more than likely they had inadvertently just hit the right sequence of key pad buttons. After all neither of the duo seemed to be wearing their glasses. In any event it wasn't long before all five were therapeutically soaking in artificially heated tropical waters flouncing about like adolescent schoolboys on holiday.

Over the course of the next few hours Crazy Dave and Dakota Slim considered that having successfully arranged for the hot tub to actually hot tub meant that they had the right to relate some of the worst jokes known to mankind. They were awful and elicited more groans per minute than was heard at the breakfast table before the first cup of coffee. Coincidentally, or it might have been in reaction, The Driver had the most unfortunate case of flatulence known to Christendom. His four brothers cognizant of his obvious distress and discomfort chose to ignore the repeated staccato hammer like anvil blows repeatedly ringing out into the night air like Eliot Ness's machine gun. All the while and in addition was the incessant cock-a-doodle-do of wild chickens coupled to the sounds from behind every hedge of numerous insects and various song birds. It was to be a long and noisy evening.

As the evening wore on so did our intrepid searchers and occasionally it required someone to jump-start conversations by a subtle change of direction. In the interest of showing that our five were more than just good looking drunken louts, one such directional discussion change offered up by The Driver was about how clear and clean the air was on the island. In defense of this cleanest air proposition The Driver cavalierly threw out that the air was so clear and clean that one of the island's taller mountains, some forty-three hundred meters above the sea, was home to a dozen astronomical telescope stations focused on the stars. All of them being scholars it was quickly obvious that a ride to the top of the world to see for themselves would be in order and someone wrote it down on a tissue so they'd remember in the morning.

All that talk of clear air and telescopes meant they spent the next couple of hours looking heavenward. One of the benefits of the hideout being so far from the city and neighbours meant the night sky was clear and bright. While all agreed the stars were not the same as back home they did wonder if the aspect of the moon was the same. It was ultimately agreed upon that it was but that could hardly be considered definitive. By time of moonrise the group was too well on their way to an alternate consciousness to be able to adequately discern the time let alone the aspect of the moon. In fact by that point in the evening's festivities just being able to see and recognize that the light in the sky was in fact the moon was an accomplishment.

At a point even later that evening while still looking heavenward they saw a strange sight. (them that believed were looking to the heavens; them that didn't were just looking up) The stars had formed a circle around the moon and the formation was pierced by a fast-moving, blue coloured meteor. It could have been real or it could have been brought on by subliminal suggestion or by over-indulgence. In any event they all sighed "ahhhhhhhhhh" at the sight.

Since the search was to continue on the high seas on the morrow a reasonably early night had been agreed to by all, but none had agreed to a sober night. You should know that early had always meant to them what late meant to most. Daybreak approached once again before final drinks were drained to dregs allowing individuals to amble off. Dakota Slim and Harri sat up the latest discussing world events and other such weighty matters under the beautiful clear night sky and an almost full moon.

When Harri finally staggered off his *little red headed friend Helmut* offered up a cock-a-doodle-do send off. Harri muttered under his breath that he hoped the mongoose population that had been imported to control the feral chickens would soon bring a plague on *Helmut's* house. In a surprising moment of clarity Harri wondered if a new problem might be coming home to roost in the islands. The chickens had also been imported. Undoubtedly a burgeoning mongoose population would soon become a surprise to the populace. People never learn that you can't mess with Mother Nature. With those final thoughts Harri drifted off on gossamer wings.

CHAPTER 6

The day's boat trip was to be a four hour tour, not unlike Gilligan's legendary - *three hour tour*. Unhappily deep sea fishing out on the Pacific necessitated a 7:15a.m. dock arrival to adequately meet the scheduled departure time. This meant that at five to six everyone awoke to the sultry sounds of *Helmut's* cock-a-doodle-do.

None of the assembled could truly be called morning people so the now normal pre-breakfast ritual of whining, head holding and hand wringing was on display. Bravely White Rhino was the only one man enough to admit to adverse effects from the previous night's festivities. It turned out this admission was solely to give license for a pathetic display of playing for sympathy and he would go on to moan and groan, for quite some time. Possessing the patience of saints the others tolerated his moaning, but they weren't truly saints and compassion quickly ran out.

Thereupon a vote was taken and it was firmly suggested that he shut the hell up as an important decision was pending.

Their recent scientific evidentiary experience that what goes down must surely come up suggested a light breakfast of coffee and bananas would probably be best that morning. As none wished to offend the chef a committee decision was offered and quickly made in the affirmative around the kitchen counter. Once all were lightly so nourished The Driver successfully shepherd them into the truck for the tear down the mountain road. White Rhino again complained that the hectic pace was adversely affecting his constitution and begged for them to slow down; he was ignored this time like last.

Thanks to The Driver's innate skills they arrived at the quay with plenty of time to spare which was a good thing as Crazy Dave promptly wandered off into the business' retail emporium. He was actively looking for new swim fins. Actually he had been doing so almost continuously since 1971. On the previous day's walkabout he'd thought he had discovered the cheapest pair yet but chose not to buy them, just in case. On this morning in the boat yard's shop he was to locate a set fully $0.26 cheaper than those found the previous day. It was of course immediately obvious that he needed to continue looking. In the mean time the others were congregating dockside watching in wonder as White Rhino began to change colour before their very eyes.

Floating alongside the dock was a whitish boat large enough to manage ten passengers but there would only be our boys today. As they clumsily clambered aboard they were introduced to the captain, who had recently relocated from Alaska. Harri made a mental note that the captain of the dive boat had also worked the Alaskan waters. It was beginning to seem that everyone they met was from somewhere else. Everyone except The Gardiner, and he couldn't wait to go somewhere else. The rest of the crew comprised of the deckhand and a Pekinese terrier who could have resided in a tea pot.

The day would be nothing but enjoyment and adventure.

Just as they were getting settled they were instructed to remove their shoes. You might think, as they did, that it was for safety reasons, but you'd be wrong. The bald headed and greatly mustachioed captain was a meticulous sort who just didn't want anyone dirtying his deck. The deckhand was a cute little seventeen year old recently landed from Washington State. Over the course of the day Harri took it upon himself to constantly remind his leering old friends that she was in fact seventeen.

As they were taking off their shoes the captain queried each if they were bringing any bananas aboard. Trust Dakota Slim to take the opportunity to make an unwise old Armenian joke that they were all bringing one aboard. The joke of course fell as flat and lifeless as his own banana. It turned out that nautically speaking the aforementioned fruit are harbingers of ill luck and no crew worth their salt would have one aboard under any circumstances. Harri thought it wise to keep quiet around his having had one for breakfast. Privately he was unsure just how long he was going to be able to keep it from being thrown out there for all to see when once underway.

It seems the captain was quite right that bananas bring bad luck. The mere mentioning of it caused the boys to spend the balance of the day in hot conversation around if it was a gag or was truly something to be concerned with.

As the boat motored from the harbour the group unanimously decided that Harri would have the first opportunity at fishing. It was a well known secret that Harri was one of the finest anglers in Canada. The others had always lived in the shadow of his natural talent and they were rightly reluctant to showcase their own less than stellar techniques in the presence of such as he. Never mind the issue if what they considered their techniques could even be labeled as such.

It was a fine morning and they had barely reached a point a kilometer from shore when the very limber seventeen year old deckhand began repeatedly bending over at the waist to get the fishing gear sorted. Feeling oddly guilty Harri was looking out to sea when he noticed a beautiful blue green mahi-mahi in the port wake. It was hove to some thirty meters away and was boldly winking at him. He immediately shouted *"fish off the port bow"* but the immediate confused look on his companions' faces caused him to resignedly mutter *"over there to the left, for God's sake"*. He sadly shook his head at his companion's utter lack of seagoing acumen.

A few moments after the only true fisherman aboard spotted the prey the others saw the great marine beauty out on the blue sea. Pandemonium ensued; the deckhand got flustered and started to drop fishing type stuff all over the deck and the Canadians and transplanted Canadian all began to jump up and down shouting and gesticulating wildly. Only our intrepid fisherman kept his head. Now, while it was true that Harri had never fished these waters, and so was unaware of the type of fishes thereabouts he knew instinctively what was what. He kept his composure as the true sportsman will and even took the time to walk the girl back to the cabin, mop her brow with a cold pre-moistened towelette and fetch her a restorative drink. She had recently had a number of tattoos applied and likely was a little feverish. The others looked on in reverence and marveled at his zen like composure.

After calming the young filly, Harri made his way back to the fishing chair, authoritatively but gently pushing his compatriots out of the way. As he gathered the needed tools for the coming fishing lesson, his keen eye quickly noted that while lure was attached to line, line was not attached to reel. The great fish was laughing at them by this time and there being no other option Harri, with a great discus like heave hurled the lure up and out over the water. It was a magnificent hurl and it glanced off the protagonist's head. As Harri knew he would the dumb beast made a play for it. The fisherman quickly wrapped the fine line around his left index finger and proceeded to fix the hook with a savage yank that drew blood from both the hunted and the hunter. Clearly, being without benefit of rod would only make the task ahead tougher but Harri was up for it. He was after all, a true sportsman.

The laborious three hour struggle between the two great foes then began in earnest. Time and time again Harri struggled mightily to reel in the precious cargo. Hand over hand he would pull the line in, only to again and again lose ground to his valiant quarry who, repeatedly and admirably found the inner strength to fight on. Time passed inexorably slowly until the outcome was obvious to all but the fish. When the great marine monster gathered his diminished and flagging strength to make one last break for freedom the outgoing line cut through the flesh of Harri's hands, but he just laughed it off. Thankfully Crazy Dave was standing nearby with a canned Margarita.

Earlier, when in the shop reviewing the modest assortment of swim fins on offer he had come across a display of $0.99 cans of the popular readymade beverage. While he didn't personally care for the libation he could not overlook such a bargain and had purchased all the shopkeeper had on hand. Now thinking quickly he poured some of the refreshing mixture over the hands and outgoing smoking line in the hope of lessening the pain on his old friend's digits. At this point the horror of it all was too much for Dakota Slim. He swooned and keeled over (a nautical term) leaving his already emotionally drained friends dumbfounded and immobile. His prostrated form then started to roll towards the open back of the boat. The risk of his falling over the stern into the churning propellers was so great that Harri momentarily stopped the fight with the undersea leviathan. Using his free hand he pulled his old friend to safety before refocusing to the task at hand.

Respect for Harri's modesty prevents furthering the storytelling. Suffice it to say the great sea creature was ultimately overpowered and landed. The captain summarily gaffed the great beast and before you could say *have you ever been to sea Jim lad* it was shoved into a bag full of ice and the cruise continued.

Unhappily no more fish were hooked, or even sighted but the day was a great one. They spent the better part of the afternoon watching and admiring the deck girl's recent tattoos. She displayed them with vigour and a modicum of modesty that some might have considered distasteful. Our friends though were not so closed minded. To a man they had always shown a great appreciation for art for art's sake and so had no compunction in closely reviewing the body tapestry. A couple of them would go on to very closely study her two designer like halved grapefruit shaped tats.

In the end it turned out there was no need for a repeat of the first day's exercise of feigning sea-sickness. Dakota Slim and later White Rhino both being overcome by the excitement of the fish epi-sode made play-acting moot.

They docked just after noon and the catch was quickly dispatched into fillets by the deckhand, the gleaming knife flashing brightly in the Hawaiian sun. This so whetted the appetites of the fellows that they stopped at the first available restaurant and it happened to be right in the boatyard. Immediately upon sitting down they hid the plastic garbage bag containing twenty kilograms of freshly filleted mahi-mahi beneath the table. They would have taken more fish but it was all they could carry. That said they were afraid that if the bounty was com-mon knowledge the chef would commandeer it to feed the entire restaurant. Americans are known worldwide for their socialist sensibilities. After each but the ever modest Harri bragged of the catch to the waitress they enjoyed a hearty lunch and a few glasses of ale.

After dining the physically and spiritually exhausted troop headed back to their hole in the wall to spend the afternoon getting primed for the evening. At some fleeting sober moment late in the day it was decided to cook up a feast for dinner. So a quick run downhill was made for groceries and admittedly more gin. It was decided that portions of the fillets yielded from the beast Harri had single handedly dragged aboard at great danger to his well being were to be grilled by White Rhino and Dakota Slim, along with some left over steak. The spectacular breakfasts they'd been partaking of made it quite clear that The Driver had become quite the gourmet in the intervening years and his offer to suchi-ize some of the catch was well received. Harri would prepare potatoes and corn while Crazy Dave would do what he did best, supervise and control arrangements. A gigantic BBQ was inexplicably dragged some thirteen meters by White Rhino to a spot he considered more conducive and they all dived into the task of preparing the evening meal. It turned out to be a feast of almost biblical proportions.

The camaraderie that they had all felt since arrival was now even greater than ever. This in spite of some fretting and lingering resentment over the successful manner in which the main course had been provided.

Relaxation and general over consumption was again the order of the evening. The hot tub performed faultlessly as did the pool. Much quicker than usual the evening gave way to the gin soaked smoky purpled hazed alternate reality our heroes had begun to look forward to. It must be obvious and it was so acknowledged by the participants that sobriety at any point during days past and those yet to come had and would be fleetingly accidental. There was a real danger that the search was being overlooked.

Conversation being an activity that required no physical energy became the only task the bunch would attempt with any sort of alacrity that evening. They went at it full tilt with raucous group discussions or with an occasional quiet conversations between two or three off to one side. As evening came on so did the breeze, for a few moments the boys considered it was raining and they were mightily confused why they weren't getting dampish. Only The Driver had discovered that the breeze in the palm fronds ten meters above their heads always sounded like that which a gentle rain made.

White Rhino and Dakota Slim, having always been the go to guys around getting things done began to feel it was their burden to re-engineer the place to better suit the group's needs. They noted jobs that needed doing and supplies that needed to be gotten. These items were jotted down on bits of paper as the thought entered their consciousness and were then left in little piles all over the house. It was their honest plan that everything was to be attempted and completed on the morrow but attention spans being what they were, well, you can imagine the outcome. The Driver, while oblivious to their suggestions seemed to accept that there was nothing he could do to hinder their undertakings so bemusedly let it carry on.

As the day's festivities drew to the inevitable close it became apparent that four decades on all of the boys had at one time or another been in love with The Driver's sister, the lovely Lisa. That night most of them passed to the other realm with thoughts of ... *Oh, what might have been.*

CHAPTER 7

ari couldn't speak for the others but he'd slept like a king, although he had got up in the middle of the night seeking another blanket which by morning he'd kicked off. Staring bleary eyed into the bathroom mirror the metro-sexual noted that the tropical climate was so moist that one seemed constantly refreshed. Hair and skin were softer, finger and toe nails seemed to grow before your eyes and cracked skin suddenly wasn't, and man could you breathe.

He wandered from his modest accommodation on the far side of a remote garage and quietly entered the house just after 9:00a.m. Most were up but there was little in the way of movement, other than White Rhino off in a corner complaining yet again of a headache he couldn't explain. Even after all the years he never did put together that if you boozed hard all night your head would willingly remind you the next morning. Back dropping this was the sound of a buzz-saw reverberating throughout the house. The sounds were nothing more than the quaint noises The Driver made whilst reposed but the racket was giving Dakota Slim flashbacks to a prison break he'd almost undertaken years earlier. At the time he was temporarily residing at the pleasure of Her Majesty within Headingly Gaol, the unhappy result of a minor misunderstanding around possession of a medicinal herb.

Once upon a time a portable cross-cut saw had been brilliantly constructed from the fossilized remains of a plesiosaur's spine by Crazy Dave and Teacher. They had unearthed the beastly fossil while burying a little problem in the sandy loam of the Manitoba Escarpment near the bustling metropolis of Morden in the early 80's. The makeshift saw had been smuggled to Dakota Slim at his temporary residence piece by piece over the course of two years less a day. The pieces were cunningly secreted within home baked cupcakes. The subterfuge had been accomplished with the unknowing aid of the kind hearted Mrs. Kuryk. This woman had been more than a school marm to Dakota Slim. She'd spent most of her life trying to keep him out of trouble. Sometimes she won, sometimes she lost, but she'd always found him as adorable as a cabbage roll and would do anything for her Sweet Baboo.

After diligently eating the cupcakes Dakota Slim would cleverly hide the individual pieces upon his person or to be more accurate, within his person. When the last piece had been delivered he painstakingly reconstructed the fossilized dinosaur into the workable tool and then laboured day and night on the cell's bars for months. Naturally, as these things always go, the night before the bars would have parted like the Red Sea he was released for good behavior. Ever since any sort of sawing drove him mad which made renovations to his recently purchased property on the island paradise of Roatan somewhat problematic.

Elsewhere, out on the patio and now taking the morning sun, Crazy Dave had been busy. In addition to being the go to guy for security he was also their computer whiz. In some magically way known only to himself he'd determined how to access the ether net and had contacted Teacher out in the midst of the Arabian Desert. Their missing companion was on a mission to bring the local population into the 21st century whether they wished it or not. This contact with the old comrade was great news and a wonderful way to start the day. They spent way too much time catching up with the friend who couldn't make the trip. You would have thought Skype service was free the way they endlessly chattered away.

The gang then sat around the living room enjoying the morning breeze while shooting the breeze over pots of coffee. This meant that at any given time at least one of them was heading or returning from the bathroom. They were all, or soon would be taking advantage of the Canada Pension Plan after all. It was testament to their friendship how quickly they slid back into what they were all those years ago. It was almost like roles in a play, everyone knew their lines and where they were supposed to be and no cues were ever missed. They were happy to see each other and each totally accepted who and what the others were. No fights, no unfriendly questions, no egos, just friends. They were like birds of paradise in paradise.

During a moment when Harri was leaning back enjoying listening to his old friends' jabber away he had a flashback to an old television program called Adventures in Paradise. Gardiner McKay had played a free spirited captain who sailed the South Seas looking for adventure on his two-masted wooden bark the Tiki. McKay had retired to Hawaii, where just after the millennium he died. He'd not been much older than those in that living room that morning and the thought left Harri cold for a moment.

Once all the coffee was drunk and the rehash of the previous days adventures were rehashed uncertain plans were made to continue the search. The one thing that all agreed upon was that boats were not to be involved. The ruse of feigning seasickness had lost its charm and humour and White Rhino who had played along for two days was exhausted. Only The Driver had not assumed the role on either trip on the bounding main. He had always been uncomfortable playing any role outside his own.

Nothing had yet been decided for the coming day and in a flash of genius Dakota Slim realized they needed to stop over thinking things. He insisted that the five jump to it and complete the daily tasks necessary to keep the house running on an even keel. The classically trained psychologist of the group reckoned if they just stopped thinking something would be bound to come to them. This seemed an odd approach but they had nothing to lose. It didn't work and in fact went the wrong way entirely.

Out of guilt a couple of them decided to repay their unknown hosts by focusing on the one or two small things that had been uncovered that were deemed fixable. To be honest they were contemplating things they'd likely broken. Thinking this sort of thing would give away their presence The Driver was dead set against it but was so laid back he acquiesced, in part just to shut them up. His mantra had always been, *things will get done when they get done and it likely makes little difference one way or the other anyway.* It was a bit longer than a more traditional mantra. A lifetime philosophy is a tough thing to change, especially when it'd worked so well for years. So he just leaned back on the comfortable couch, closed his eyes, started chanting his mantra and drifted away.

Much time was wasted trying to find things to fix that were within their limited abilities to do so and a couple of hours later they realized they'd accomplished nothing. Throwing their arms up in acknowledgement of defeat the intrepid group piled into the Toyota and headed off to a park on the shore some distance from Kona. The Driver was hoping exposure to some traditional island culture would capture their limited attention span for a short time.

But first, a drive through the little village that had first attracted The Driver to source out the hideaway in the first place. The village was known locally as Holualoa, to be honest it was known everywhere as Holualoa because that was the village's name. There was not much of note in the quaint little place other than a few shops, bars and a rundown hotel but it was famous for a longtime business operation that made authentic ukuleles. If a soul had nine hours over the course of a week the proprietor would help you make your own instrument. You'll recall White Rhino had purchased *a genuine Hawaiian ukulele, handmade in Malaysia* a few days earlier. In his mind this meant he was now armed him with an expert's knowledge. He proceeded to enlighten the rest of the boys on the ins and outs of the intriguingly complex instrument. After that annoying and rather self-serving discourse a more pleasant half hour was spent wandering the small shop while White Rhino was interrogating the owner. No purchases were made but business cards with the instrument's four or five main chords printed on the reverse were surreptitiously spirited out of the shop.

Motoring further down the road they came across a small antique shop chock-a-block full of interesting bric-a-brac. Putting it kindly, the Crew to a man were well known as being somewhat thrifty so such an establishment could not be bypassed. As an aside it was rumoured that Crazy Dave and Dakota Slim had invented copper wire by arguing over a penny that neither one was prepared to release. Once inside the shop they split up to search out things of value that had been missed by the those less talented than themselves, much to the consternation of the middle aged frumpy shop owner. All she could see was five grizzled bleary eyed lay-a-bouts invading her premises and she was afraid the place was about to be plucked clean. Naturally nobody bought anything although there were many interesting tid-bits on offer. An ancient wood and steel Red Comet sled hanging on the outside wall caught their eyes. How the sled got to be in Hawaii was a mystery that was discussed ad-nauseam for much of the afternoon. The Driver and Crazy Dave tried mightily to put an end to the line of discourse by insinuating that snow occasionally fell in the mountains. The suggestion that Hawaii had enough regular snowfall to entice retailers to import sleds from the mainland fell on cloth ears and the debate raged on.

Next up on the magical mystery tour was spiritual bread for the soul. The refuge known as Honaunau had once been Royal grounds and had traditionally provided refuge to lawbreakers. They were Royal grounds no more. Around the turn of the 20th century the freedom and fun loving Americans came to unchain the native peoples from the anarchy and despotic rule of the islands' hereditary kings. Americans, then and now, have no stomach for people being oppressed by any type of government that they happen to disapprove of, at the time. The Royal family was soon out and the Americans quickly began to show the poor downtrodden islanders just how lucky they were. But I digress.

In the good old Hawaiian days if a law breaker could reach the refuge at Honaunau he'd be safe from legal repercussions for any transgression that may have knowingly or unknowingly been committed. The Driver momentarily harboured the thought that this might be just the place for the five of them to live out their time. At such a place they could be free from the fear of retribution for things that some insisted they had allegedly done. Alas, it wasn't to be. You couldn't get a glass of beer to save your life so any potential protection from the Man was not worth the self denial.

There was a bit of bother on that lovely sunny afternoon visit. While clambering about the lava covered shore White Rhino saw a turtle in the water. He'd had an affinity for the creatures since grade school when his parents had given him a small painted turtle for his 7th Christmas. Being hard to tell with turtles he promptly named him, or she Rocky. He had always been slightly myopic and thought Santa Claus had brought him a flying squirrel. He kept Rocky in the left pocket of his pastel green TK's as he hop-scotched off with Crazy Dave to *The Sisters of Have Mercy and Don't Whip Me So* Catholic elementary school they'd attended for ten years. Neither had been particularly gifted scholars.

When White Rhino spied the slumbering creature wallowing in the surf he lunged for the great testudine and slipped and fell to his knees on the black lava. The rocks were like sandpaper covered in broken glass and he screamed in pain like a little girl. Similar situations had arisen numerous times over a lifetime of White Rhino's futile attempts at proving his manhood. Normally something so foolish would have generated hours of mirth for the rest of them but not today. As a group they were not happy with the scene White Rhino had made as too many people had taken notice. Their short stay at Honaunau was over and they quickly and not too gently carried him back to the truck. One of the knees in question had already swollen to the size of a passion fruit and would shortly grow to the size of one of the large delicious oranges that grew on the grounds just outside their hideaway.

Ever prepared The Driver had a backup plan around where they could lay low for the rest of the day. He had also wisely envisioned that they might have need of a conveyance or two. The clever man had sagely arranged for two kayaks and a paddle board to be on hand in the garage at the house. In anticipation of such an eventuality as had now occurred he had loaded them into the rear of the truck at first light.

Since the boys came from the frigid North Country The Driver knew controlling of kayaks and paddle boards would be inbred in their DNA. That was fair enough but it had been years since any of them had been out in a kayak hunting walrus and it was a skill set that needed practice with some regularity. It was to be the only mistaken thought he'd had about his friends in quite some time, other than actually extending the invitation to visit the island in the first place.

Once they had loaded the prostate form that was White Rhino into the back of the Toyota they headed off to a deserted beach The Driver knew of. The spot was quite near where Captain Cook had first come ashore. It was also the place where parts of him would remain after becoming the catch of the day. Life truly is a bitch. Captain Cook ended up bobbing about with half a dozen turnips in a stew pot when all he had to do was to walk over to Honaunau and he would have been safe. Harri made a point of pointing out that said captain had been born and grew up very near the North Sea coastal birth home of himself, for what that was worth.

After a tortuous drive down a meandering dirt road the beach they were headed to proved heaven on earth. The road ended alongside the water and the boys quickly threw the watercraft into the surf. White Rhino, The Driver and Crazy Dave paddled them straight out to sea then turned left along the coast to the deserted sand spit that was to be their afternoon's respite. The Driver had anticipated their exertions would produce a great thirst so in addition to the watercraft he'd also packed away a cooler load of refreshments. He once again looked a genius to his friends. It was left to Dakota Slim and Harri to manhandle the unwieldy refreshment cooler along the dirt track past a number of small cottages facing the raging Pacific.

It would be a wonderful afternoon on the water although Crazy Dave was reluctant to remain above the surface for too long. He knew he presented too good a target for anyone watching. Most of his time beneath the waves was spent trying desperately to catch one of the numerous fish sashaying about. The water was so clear he could frustratingly see them frolicking ten meters away. Truth be told he was still put out with Harri's success and wanted to catch something, anything, to prove that he was as good an angler. It would be all for naught and he failed miserably in providing a bounty for his friends. By this time White Rhino's knee had swollen to the size of a medium sized cantaloupe and it was decided that a cold beer bottle applied to the appendage would be therapeutic. There had been a close vote to cut the leg off with a broken bottle but a thin majority deemed it impractical. They were all loath to risk damaging the pristine environment with broken glass. Harri had been secretly hoping they would elect to utilize the Swiss Army Knife he'd been carrying for decades in hopes of such an opportunity arising. Alas the Crew thought this impractical as well. Besides how would he have walked out on just one leg?

Once the vote was formally accepted into the minutes it was Dakota Slim and Harri's turn in the kayaks. They were quickly pulled out to the deep by a vicious rip-tide that would have terrified the more experienced. Our two hadn't the skill or wit to be concerned so they just floated about watching waves and a small tsunami that was headed their way. Through sheer determination, grit and ignorance they held on to their respective craft while those on shore looked on in rapture. Ignorance being bliss they had absolutely no concern for their well being as they bobbed about with views of hills rising up from the beach ringing the small bay and the great expanse of the Pacific going on out forever. A sudden squall came up and The Driver who'd always had a weak constitution dug a hole in the sand with his bare hands in which to stick his head and calm his fears. Once it started to rain heavily the two out on the water headed for shore and would later recount how wonderfully alone one felt so close to the ocean's surface.

The place was magically serene. Walking the sand, paddling the boats, splashing in the surf and snorkeling were just what the doctor ordered, that and a few cold ones. The cold ones had momentarily presented a problem. Seemingly the greatest and only super power left on the planet had yet to discover the beauty and convenience of twist off beer caps. As was their wont the group always relied heavily on the semi-cleverness of White Rhino to anticipate most eventualities. True to form he had brought a hat to the island with a built in bottle opener, genius. Unhappily the weight of prodigious drinking and other stuff had clotted what was left of his mind and he had forgotten the hat that morning. It was left to Dakota Slim and a lifetime experience with beer bottles to devise an ingenious method of using one bottle to open another and saved the day.

After the sudden squall had ended the strangely eerie calm was broken by the sight on the high seas of a solitary surfer motionless astride his board. He hadn't moved for some minutes and while some may have considered he was awaiting the perfect wave the group was instantly on the razor's edge. There is no easy way to put this. They panicked and decided to make a break for it just in case. Three went off with the watercrafts while Dakota Slim and Harri were charged with taking the flotsam of the day back to the truck. Dakota Slim went first to ensure no one was waiting for them and naturally he wished to be unencumbered while doing so. He quickly moved up the pathway as the other three pushed out to sea. Harri as usual was left to carry the load.

It happened then. A striking middle-aged blond beach babe clad in a green bikini that cared little that it barely covered her ample bosom was coming up the path walking an Irish setter towards Harri. This was the second green bikini encountered that seemed insufficient for its intended load. She was swaying her hips as only an island woman can and Harri was flummoxed. He didn't know where to look;

bosom, hips, eyes which were a stunning green that matched her bikini, or the contrasting coloured Irish setter. For a second it crossed his mind it could be a trap but dismissed that quickly as she was clearly enamoured of his good looks. As she passed by close enough for him to catch the delightful fragrance of her *Dove, Damage Therapy Volume Boost Shampoo* he stubbed his toe on a wayward black volcanic rock in the path. The pain would have felled a rhinoceros but he stood his ground and through a grimace smiled hello and continued on with a single tear in his eye. A tear shed for a lost opportunity, not the pain. It would turn out he'd broken the toe thus proving yet again no good deed goes unrewarded.

Once back at the truck wet trunks were changed for dry clothes behind some trees and Dakota Slim unseemingly spent more time than required being naked to the wind. Stuff was quickly loaded and water craft were secured to the state of the art truck racks designed solely for the purpose of safely securing such things. They were quickly on their way down the tortuous path to the main road. While descending a particularly dangerous stretch of the goat path that would have had a normal person terrified to the point of inaction disaster struck. A red securing strap decided to stop providing its sole reason for being. It snapped with the crack of a pistol shot. Could it have been a pistol shot?

All the boys knew for sure was that one of the kayaks fired forward over the front of the truck then took a hard right and sheared the mirror off the passenger door like a knife going through crunchy peanut butter. Brakes were hammered on, four doors opened and ten hands attacked the situation that had offended all. In no time the damage was assessed and a plan of action was sorted out. How could something not have been quickly sorted with that collection of geniuses standing about? The load was quickly re-configured and re-secured and they were soon on their way again only this time Dakota Slim spent the balance of the journey with his window open hanging on to a mirror that was clinging to life by one thin wire.

As they approached town twenty minutes later The Driver wisely pulled over to recheck the load. At the very spot he indiscriminately chose to pull over was a half eaten banana strategically placed on a rock so as to be impossible to miss. Bananas truly are bad luck as the sight of it set the argument off once again.

They hadn't yet found what they were searching for but they all secretly knew it was close by. Each was confident it would reveal itself if they could just focus.

Eat and drink was by then the only order of the day. Except for Crazy Dave, who would only swill that Primo crap they'd been downing the local Kona beer since arrival. The clever Kona Brewing Company had considered some time back that if they opened a restaurant adjacent to where they made the beer they would have a captive audience. It was a brilliant idea as proved by The Driver who had been there numerous times. They now headed there as quickly as posted speed limits allowed.

Immediately upon arrival at the eatery White Rhino leapt from his shotgun vantage point to assure a table as soon as possible. Only to immediately collapse on the roadway in spasms of agony. He was so hungry he had forgotten his knee. One would have considered this unlikely as the offending member had now swollen to a watermelon size dimension, but he was really hungry. Parking space was at a premium so they had to leave him lying in the road, but only for a moment or two while they grabbed a spot that just opened up. Once parked they collected White Rhino off the roadway and entered the establishment like they owned the place. They immediately belly upped to the bar and it wasn't a few moments gone when one of them noticed an empty table with a reserved sign. Naturally they sat down and almost immediately some smart mouthed citizen at an adjoining table loudly questioned what right they had to sit there. Before anything could develop Crazy Dave wisely dragged them all outside to the establishment's legendary al-fresco dining experience.

Sensing trouble the staff immediately located a table for the boys. They were quickly seated and all settled down for a couple of hours of refreshment and relaxation. A friendly, though chunky, waitress would go on to provide unending glasses of beer and something called gourmet designer pizzas.

The reserved table incident in the bar had not gone unnoticed and twice over the ensuing hours the manager wandered by to chat and make sure there were no hard feelings and that everyone was having a good time.

The joint's manager had weird eyes that rolled around inside his head like marbles in a glass jar. The boys found it disconcerting to look at him as he regaled them with the recitation of his résumé of dozens of bar manager jobs he'd held over the past few years. He also jabbered on in a weird rambling transcendental conversation with himself around some sort of Korean Karaoke bar with accommodating hostesses that only The Driver seemed to grasp the context of. The manager's obvious difficulty in maintaining a line of conversation for more than a second or two likely explained why he'd been unable to hold a job for any length of time. In a brief moment free of his pain induced delirium White Rhino opined it might have had something to do with his being from Tennessee. No one was quite sure where their friend had come up with Tennessee.

Later Crazy Dave would vehemently point out that there had been no offer of the usual courtesy of a free drink. It was clear to all his meager funds were fast running out.

A mongoose suddenly ran across the floor beneath their table and it was like a light switch flicked. Nobody they had met, with the exception of The Gardiner, came from here. The restaurant manager was maybe from Tennessee and was definitely recently arrived from Germany, the chunky waitress Annabelle was from Oklahoma, the grapefruit bedecked deck-girl was from Washington, both boat captains hailed from Alaska, another helper on the dive boat called Michigan home. What was going on? None of the lads considered it coincidence, something was up. As sure as spring follows winter their cover had been blown.

It crossed their addled minds that Shady Norm might be the source of the leak so they unanimously committed themselves to head right over to his place of business, once they finished eating of course. In another link of the chain of never ending coincidences his diving emporium stood right next door to a Korean karaoke bar. Seeing the coincidence for what it was they quickly put together a plan involving a drink in the bar with a Korean lovely on each knee whilst pumping Shady Norm for info. Or was it Shady Norm on the knee and pumping Korean lovelies? It had been a confusing evening up to that point and it looked like it would continue to be so.

Everything immediately fell apart when it was discovered Shady Norm's place was shut tighter than a tart's heart. The Driver being reluctant to give up easily on a fine plan, rolled down his window and asked a passerby and his lovely lady of the evening if either had any idea where Shady Norm might be. This was not as farfetched as it might seem. The guy had the look of someone who might have followed Shady Norm's habits. His eyes were wide and staring with a strange back lit glow to them that was a trifling unnerving. The gibberish he spewed about where to find Shady Norm and/or Korean lovelies was unintelligible. The three in the back of the truck began to panic and insisted on getting away from there as fast as possible. The Driver accommodated by peeling away while the man in the street shouted after them in derision, "*what, no tip you freakin' howlies*".

Relieved they returned to the house on the hill and immediately upon arrival tried to fix the broken mirror that had earlier been guillotined by the wayward kayak. Nearly everyone had an idea on how to accomplish the task. The hard truth was that after numerous days of denying self-denial they barely had enough functioning brain cells between them to figure out how to put on White Rhino's bottle opener equipped hat. Sadly it was like the blind leading the blind. An apt metaphor since it was already as black as pitch out. They soon all collapsed in defeat on the patio after somehow wisely agreeing that trained professionals would be required.

Once again the festivities went well on into the night as they continued down the road of a recently discovered secondary search. The much easier search for self-consciousness, or was that self-discovery. It doesn't really matter.

Before losing the necessary where-with-all, that he knew in his heart was pending, Harri managed to send the agreed upon coded message to his loved one – *still alive and well* – utilizing Crazy Dave's electronic gizmo. He hoped it would confound any trackers but did wonder if it was all for naught.

CHAPTER 8

Awakened early by a gaggle of chickens outside the window Harri spent some time pondering the weather while awaiting his head to clear and his eyes to focus. Every day the same thing; sunny at 6:00a.m., cloudy four hours later, showers at 4:00 then clear again at 10:00p.m. with constant warm temperatures. It was so boringly dull compared to back home.

The plans for the day began with breakfast of leftover steak accompanying the now routine *omelet d'Driver* and a cornucopia of handpicked fruit. Lingering over coffee the group agreed to a gentle wander around Kona in deference to White Rhinos' still slightly swollen knee. This would be followed by a swim in the blue Pacific at a spot up the coast. This would be followed by a drive to the top of a mountain to confirm the clean air hypotenuse relentlessly being put forward by The Driver. Between mouthfuls of his namesake omelet The Driver had cautioned that t-shirts and shorts would be woefully insufficient at the top of the world.

Outside in the tropical garden of delights the feral males of the local Gallus Gallus Domesticus crowed constantly throughout breakfast. It was almost as if they were sending out messages.

Eventually accomplishing the daily challenge of all moving in sync towards one goal the boys, without malice aforethought, changed the plan. They shortly ended up in the crowded parking lot outside the other main dive shop in Kona. Some of them thought it would be wise to do another comparison of Shady Norm's competitor on the QT. It wasn't that majority ruled within the little group; rather, once a plausible proposition for action was put forward by anyone they were like the Three Musketeers, one for all an all for one. It was the way it had always been and seldom did anything get accomplished. Even the Communists knew you need to have someone in charge.

Once at the shop and to a hearty round of applause Crazy Dave finally bought some flippers. White Rhino also did the retail thing and killed two birds with one stone, picking up some defense and an underwater accessory at the same time. He purchased a knife with a half meter long blade which could be used to fend off under water sharks or the above water kind. It could also come in handy for roasting a weenie or putting peanut butter on a piece of toast.

It had become brutally hot as they finally meandered towards the beach The Driver had picked out for them. Ever thirsting for knowledge, and the opportunity to show off, Dakota Slim utilized his watch and the angle of the sun to announce they were headed in a southerly direction. He would later use a similar trick with his Timex to determine the elevation at the top of the mountain. It turned out the beach they were headed to was northward; it was only a $10 watch.

They were destined for Waipio Beach by way of the town of Waimea. The town name struck a chord and it wasn't long before in best ABBA styling's, someone quipped *why nota mea* to which in perfect harmony the reply was the obvious *why nota youa*. There would be a quick stop in the town to load up on fluids because the ever present danger of dehydration had remained forefront in their thoughts since their arrival on the island. Before he had left home White Rhino's mother had repeatedly warned him of the danger, and that motherly concern had created an almost pathological fear in him of succumbing to the curse. It was frankly a worry to all of them and they paid extraordinary attention and took every opportunity to protect themselves from its dire effects, even if it meant drinking beer early in the day. Once well stocked with a barley based elixir purchased from a local green grocer they travelled on.

When they arrived at the lookout over the wilderness beach there was a guard post and a sign indicating there would be no driving down from the four hundred meter elevation to the beach below unless by way of a four wheeled drive vehicle. As usual The Driver had anticipated every contingency. With a jaunty wave of his hand to the Establishment's representative they headed down the seventy degree incline for the quarter of an hour trip to the jungle below. The Driver's fingers soon started squeezing the steering wheel so tight plastic oozed between his digits. He suddenly and quite hoarsely suggested a quick stop for pictures. The others seeing the fear in his eyes, the slight twitching at the right corner of his mouth and the small stream of escaping saliva accepted the suggestion for what it was. They all tumbled out to snap some snaps.

By time they reached the bottom of the precipitous cliff all were emotionally exhausted but they still needed to buck up again. There was now the impregnable jungle undergrowth to overcome. The space between trees was so narrow it was a fortuitous thing that the mirror on the passenger door had recently been summarily sheared off. Passage through the dense foliage would not have been possible if it had still been in place. The truck traversed over logs hiding nesting vipers and forded across water filled potholes teeming with malaria infused mosquitoes. Dakota Slim claimed these latter were similar in size to that of the legendary Edmonton flying badger. While maneuvering through the hellish path they noticed two or three cars hanging in the mantle of trees above them obviously having failed in the downward passage. They were on their sides or roofs with the skeletons of the foolhardy still visible as a warning to others. Harri surreptitiously made the sign of the cross. He was sensibly worried his companion's godless ways would shortly rain fire down upon them. They would need all the help they could muster for the day ahead.

The truck burst from the jungle like a cruise missile and landed after a couple of bounces on the rocky tree lined kilometer long beach. Waves were crashing relentlessly along the length of the volcanic black sand and it was as magnificent as Teri Hatcher's chest. There were only a half a dozen souls on the expanse of sand along with what appeared to be a beached sperm whale. On closer inspection the whale turned out to be a vacationing banker enjoying the sun. The water was too dangerous to enjoy but trunks were put on anyway. As with the previous beach adventure this was accomplished amongst the trees and again, disturbingly, it seemed to take Dakota Slim ten minutes to remove his shorts and put on his trunks. After witnessing the graphically uncomfortable display each of the group needed to be alone. Splitting up they wandered off in different directions.

Harri had some stomach discomfit so thought it best to walk some distance down the beach. His explanations that the sounds the others had been hearing were just ducks quacking no longer pacified his companions. The beach's thirty meter wide wonderful hot soft black sand was so saturated that he found that even four meters from the water's edge he'd sink up to his ankles. Halfway along he came across a wide freshwater river running to the ocean. This warm water was moving very fast and the river bed was strewn with large rocks and boulders which made for treacherous footing. This was compounded by the sea's crashing surf meeting freshwater in a boiling cauldron exactly where Harri had unwisely chosen to ford. The force of the opposing torrents caused him to slip in the middle of the river bed. Upon regaining his footing and after coming up for air he was facing an inland view that could be best described as Jurassic Park like. The valley he was looking up went on for some distance and he could see the point where the steep hills moved together to meet on opposite shores of the narrow river. It was a beautiful scene.

Once safely across the raging stream the walk to the end of the deserted sand beach was glorious. The beach ended abruptly at another four hundred meter sheer rock face and he took a whizz at the precise point where sand, cliff and sea met. Heading back he met White Rhino and Crazy Dave headed towards the same cliff for possibly the same reason he'd been. Moments later Dakota Slim appeared but he was headed for a shapely bikini clad Germanic intellectual offering advice on how to best navigate the treacherous waters of the river crossing. Dakota Slim would always go out of his way to take sage advice from Western European strangers, especially if bikini clad. Harri noticed this bikini wasn't green.

When they had all finished their assorted tramping they returned to the starting point and The Driver. They found him stretched out on the soft sand with his ear to the ground and eyes closed in concentration, possibly listening for something. He was surrounded by a number of empty beer bottles that must have been unearthed by rogue waves as they weren't there when the boys had wandered off. They all had raging thirsts by this time and when Crazy Dave opened the cooler he was startled to find there was little beer within. In a plausible explanation The Driver mused they must have forgotten to put them all in when they'd been purchased or possibly they'd left some in the shopping cart. Always fully accepting whatever The Driver said without question they nodded in unison before quickly and efficiently disposing of the few bottles on hand. In addition to thirst they all needed to settle their nerves pending the return journey up the mountain. The ride up seemed more hazardous and thrilling than the ride down. At times the truck seemed headed straight up.

There is something about exertion, even when sitting, which stimulates the appetite. As they passed again through Waimea they pulled over at the local Burger King for a modest takeout repast to enjoy while driving on to the top of the world. As they rode along, stuffing their faces with the nutritious processed food, they contemplated again that the thrusting peak of Mauna Kea was reportedly forty-three hundred meters above the beach they'd just left. The elevation would be later confirmed, more or less by Dakota Slim's Timex. They had a longish ride ahead of them so all but The Driver settled back and relaxed. It was hoped they'd arrive as the sun set over the neighbouring island of Maui and Crazy Dave, in particular, was looking forward to the reputed cleanest air on the planet. He had spent eons pretending to work by shaking dockage and determining the value of Number 1 Red Northern in dark and dusty out of the way grain elevators throughout the Canadian Prairies. He was looking forward to breathing clean air once again.

In no time at all they were travelling along the wonderfully pothole free Hawaiian highways and The Driver contemptuously passed all traffic that insisted on obeying posted speed signs. He did so with a derogatory comment for each and every car passed, usually accompanied by a glare at the driver and his fist raised in full shake. Even though concentrating hard on the driving he still had the courtesy to pass on his limitless knowledge of their destination. They learned that many countries utilized the various telescopes at the summit of the mountain to closely map the celestial universe, also keeping an eye out for any rogue Klingons headed earth's way. Being ever suspicious White Rhino, in spite of his near constant reading of scientific magazines from the cold war era, voiced that he intended to ensure that the spying telescopes were all truly pointed heavenward and not at his bedroom window.

The trip that afternoon covered a great deal of the Big Island's diverse terrain. The lowlands close to the sea appeared very similar to the treeless barren high plains of New Mexico. This scrubby rolling land had expansive areas fenced off allowing goats and cows to go where they wished while preventing mankind from doing the same. The pickup spent a long time passing by the Parker Ranch at one hundred and twenty kilometers an hour. Moving inland the slow climb skyward started and vegetation became more decidedly tropical. Later still as they rose ever higher, the trees and other greenery started to remind them of the west coast of North America. They were amongst large stands of towering cedar like trees all clumped impregnably close together.

After a couple of hours they were approaching a clearly discernible peak on the relentless climb to the heavens. The vegetation began to get sparse until even ground cover disappeared. Large areas were covered by the tumbled black rock they now knew to be ancient lava flow. In addition to being suspicious of nearly everything White Rhino was also a conspiracy theorist and he voiced that this desolate spot was clearly where they had faked the lunar landing. As usual no one would comment on yet another of his nonsensical pronouncements against authority and science.

When they turned off the main highway onto the gravel track at the base of the mountain it was cloudy, cloudy enough to enforce traveling at modestly safe speeds which irritated The Driver no end. He was much too good at the controls to drive slowly and he beat that poor Toyota like a red headed stepson. They were either ascending into the clouds or the clouds were descending upon them but whichever the outcome was the same. They could barely see the windshield wipers on the other side of the glass. The drive had become dangerous and tensions were rising in the front while in the back White Rhino prattled on about how the government was screwing the working man. This was a bit of a laugh really as he hadn't worked a day in his life. They passed a Ranger Station about halfway up the targeted mountain but motored quickly passed in the rush to arrive on the summit at sunset. It was a decision they would come to rue.

Suddenly they popped above the clouds. They could see forever, as long as they didn't look toward the sun. It was so bright as to make it impossible to see where they were going. That circuitous route around the countless dizzying switchbacks of the mountain meant one second they were in blinding sunlight and the next in deathly dark blackness of shadow caused by the mountain blocking out the sun. Each carried a similar danger.

One side of the road hewn from the ancient volcano was a sheer drop thousands of meters to certain death and the other was a solid granite wall that a mere glancing blow would have resulted in careening off into oblivion. Undeterred The Driver continued on with pedal to the metal. He fishtailed that truck back and forth up the dusty gravel path that even a mountain goat would have been unable to traverse without a calming dose of valium and a Seeing Eye dog. Self preservation required that something be done to protect themselves from blinding white sunlight one moment and pitch black the next. It fell to Dakota Slim to hang his head out the window and scream out the distance to the edge of the precipice. He was like some 19th century deckhand on a Mississippi paddle wheeler shouting *Mark Twain* to the captain to ensure safe passage.

They reached the summit in the nick of time and were met by the sight of hordes of sightseers. All around the crest of the mountain were tour buses disgorging Japanese tourists holding Nikon cameras. *"Didn't they once try to bomb this place back to the Stone Age"* Harri quietly queried the others?

Immediately as they parked amongst the nest of ten million dollar celestial observatories nestled on the roof of the world The Driver's earlier suggestion of long pants hit home. He had never been one to buck convention and the boys had considered it was just his usual decorum and modesty that had brought forth that early morning dress-code like suggestion. It turned out that it wasn't just his natural inclination to be well dressed. Rather it was because it was cold at the summit, brutally cold, and that was saying a lot. They all hailed from the great white north and so had some good idea of what cold was. Just a few scant hours previous they had been walking on a black sand beach at 30C and now forty-three hundred meters above the sea the temperature was barely the freezing point of water. It was a shock to their systems. Harri put on three shirts as well as pants atop his shorts and the others were not far off. White Rhino went one step further by wrapping himself in a couple of beach towels. Crazy Dave began to shiver uncontrollably.

They were there for a reason and The Driver had no intention of missing any of it after all he'd gone through to get them there. He was like a border collie the way he rounded them up and moved them all to the guard rail at the side of the road. The Crew all stood reverently as the moon rose over the shadow cast by Mauna Kea. Looking down from their perch all that could be seen was the solid rock of mountain dropping away a thousand meters and disappearing into a pillowy white blanket of clouds. It was a strange sensation to be above clouds and not aboard an airplane. The boys were all scratching their heads at this point as they thought they'd come to see the sunset in the west over Maui not the moon rise in the east. The Driver had known all along that the moon rose before the sun set at the summit. He'd kept it to himself to see if any of them would notice, they didn't.

Then almost simultaneously the boys started to feel odd. They were unable to catch their breath and their thinking was impaired, not that being thinking impaired was in itself odd for this bunch. Suddenly with no warning Harri needed relief in a big way and looking about he could determine no evidence of washroom facilities for the admiring public. While all the buildings' upper doors were opening to allow telescopic views of the heavens the doors into the buildings themselves were locked up tighter than a conservative's purse. As the herd of telescopes rotated into position with accompanying whirring and clicking Harri took the distraction as an opportunity.

He hung a rat, cheek by jowl against the side of one of the buildings hoping against hope that it wasn't the one that Canada rented. He had no thought for anything other than blessed relief and while in third shake (he had always been meticulous) Crazy Dave came storming up and incredulously voiced his concerns over the action he had just witnessed. *"Didn't you notice the hundred people with cameras milling about watching you"* he screeched like a fish wife. Then he went on to prattle something about acting like an alley cat who will take a piss whenever and wherever the notion strikes. Crazy Dave had a lot of faults but a lack of polite sensibilities had never been one and those gentlemanly sensibilities had clearly been offended. Harri was chastened and promised his old friend to be more thoughtful when publicly relieving himself in future.

A quarter of an hour later the border collie once again gathered them together to watch the sun set over an island a hundred kilometers in the distance, by all accounts Maui. That task accomplished there was little discussion around when to leave as White Rhino could no longer feel his toes. They bundled back into the truck and took a more leisurely drive down and this time stopped for acclimatization at the ranger station. During the walkabout at the stop they all immediately felt better. If only they'd taken the time to stop on the way up a couple of dozen men would not have gone to bed that night with thoughts of inadequacy after witnessing what they'd seen on that mountain top. Not to mention the wistful thoughts their wives would be having for some time to come.

The Ranger Station was very crowded and there was a small shop selling souvenirs. Crazy Dave and Dakota Slim ever on the lookout for a deal scoured the racks for something they knew not what in the hope that it would be on sale. Harri was captivated by an electronic plasma ball on a counter and he kept returning to it time and time again. The Driver and White Rhino stood to the side shaking their heads in wonder at their friends' laser like focus on the trivial. They soon needed herding again and once they'd all been moved to the out of doors they immediately came across huge lines of people waiting to take a peek at the heavens through some more reasonably sized telescopes. They masterfully feigned stupidity and pretended they didn't realize people were standing in line as they each stepped up to a telescope in turn. Harri saw the rings of Saturn at his glimpse and wouldn't shut up about it for hours. Ever the know it all and with patience running thin Crazy Dave grandly announced that you could see Saturn and its damn rings with gold plated opera glasses. The news burst Harri's balloon.

The ride home was quite subdued as they were all bagged although hearts were set to racing a number of times. The Driver had always insisted that he pass any vehicle in his path and he mistakenly felt the well loaded Toyota pickup was as responsive and nimble as an Audi R8. While it was true that both vehicles were similar in that they each had four wheels the cold hard facts were that each machines' responses to driver impetus around velocity and changes in directions were remarkably dissimilar. These realities caused some occasionally sphincter discomfort for the passengers on the return journey.

Arriving safely back at the house on the hill they took only moments to unpack the gear, throwing everything directly into the garage to await sorting on the morrow. Another evening of gin drinking commenced amongst the ever present swirling Hawaiian clouds that seemed to follow the lads everywhere. Great use continued to be made of pool, patio and hot tub which helped with the decompression from the day's travails. It must be said that the hot tub now worked seamlessly after the almost constant ministrations to its electrical system by Crazy Dave and Dakota Slim.

That evening something would occur that was more of a self fulfilling prophecy than anything else. The drunkenness and general stupefaction of the participants for much of the past few days had resulted in the odd stubbed toe and the occasional dropping of a priceless objet d'art. But by far the most common result of their lack of clarity had been the bouncing off the large screen door that led from the living room to the patio as they bounded in and out of the house like spirited Shetland ponies. They had all been guilty of rubber balling off the screen once or twice each evening and they did tend to be quite sheepish about it. Usually these events happened without witness but it had happened often enough that all were aware of the goings on.

It was not something that could be easily explained and they all had no difficulty opening and shutting the door most of the time. It was just that occasionally they would plumb forget that it was a door and it didn't help that sometimes the screen was closed and other times left ajar, or even fully open. Ensuring the door was open before stepping through just seemed to be one of those things they all had difficulty wrapping their minds around. Now it happened to all, but one of them just didn't squash his nose and shake it off before quietly sliding the door across in hopes that nobody had noticed his transgression.

Dakota Slim had other ideas around this screen door. Since thirteen when he'd first witnessed William Shatner chew up and spit out the scenery while overacting as Captain James T Kirk of the Starship Enterprise (NCC-1701) he'd believed in the other dimension. To be honest he'd searched his entire life for the gateway and since the Saturday evening past he was now convinced that the screen door was the portal to said other dimension. He'd long ago had enough of this dimension and was keen to visit the other, if only for a short period. While in his cups that first Saturday he'd made some mental calculations and was convinced that if he could just pass through the screen fast enough he could be transported to where he wanted to be. There was a problem though, having always been a failure at even basic arithmetic he had no choice but to verify his theory by scientific discovery, that being trial and error.

He was determined and had taken to surreptitiously walking into and bouncing off the screen at a steadily increasing impetus since the thought first manifested inside his cranium. All these prior tests had culminated in his now knowing exactly what warp-speed was required. Not wanting to be thirsty on the other side he'd decided to take a drink with him, and a smoke, his second of the day. Ever the showman and knowing in his heart that he was undoubtedly right he decided to make the transition through hyperspace in front of his lifelong friends.

Who better to watch him achieve the penultimate item on his bucket list?

Well, he was wrong.

It wasn't a portal to another dimension. It was just a portal to the patio. Dakota Slim encountered the screen at a speed that can only be likened to that of White Rhino's fruitless pursuits of *my little red headed friend Helmut* down the driveway. Of course the screen could not take his bulk, modest though that bulk may have been. It gave way with a mighty crash and was hurled nearly three meters out into the garden. Everyone had been watching but they were still shaken and taken aback by the violence which preceded the door leapfrogging across the patio. The Driver once again looked on with detached bemusement at what had been wrought by merely offering up a place to stay.

Once the obligatory animated group discussion of where Dakota Slim had gone wrong was fully dissected he reckoned an act of atonement was warranted. Never having been able to know when to call it a day he decided to wash the kitchen floor and as clearly as night follows day he was headed for another disaster. He inexplicably felt bottle water would do a better job than that from the tap and with his head still ringing with the failed attempt at space travel he inadvertently chose a well shaken bottle of tonic water from the stainless steel double doored refrigerator. Why the bottle was well shaken was never adequately explained but Crazy Dave was seen to have a glancing look over the top of his glasses. This was noted just prior to the resulting explosion followed almost simultaneously by a long drawn out expletive from Dakota Slim's diaphragm. The commotion was undoubtedly heard up the hill at the legendary pre-fab Vietnamese house built on a slant.

Things soon settled down to what was now passing for normal and to paraphrase that 60's oriental mystical crooner Grace Slick, they fed their heads, till the early morning hours, again.

CHAPTER 9

There was a busy and fulfilling day in the offing when the boys awoke on yet another day in paradise. The whole Hawaiian vibe was so sublime they'd recognized there was a real danger their search might be taking a back seat to their pleasant debauchery. Draining the third pot of coffee they decided to at least make an effort over the coming day.

The weather again promised to be just as they liked, sunny and warm and as they were pecking about like chickens in the kitchen there were half a dozen of the real things doing the same out on the lawn. There was also a cacophony of squawking overhead from countless other winged creatures in the trees. Like with every other morning, when breakfast was being rustled up one or two wandered out to the jungle to collect fresh fruit. The less time they spent grocery shopping lessened the risk of exposure and fruit off the vine had the added benefit of reducing out of pocket expenses. They were a most thrifty bunch, unless White Rhino had built up a head of steam in which case he could blow through cash like shit through a goose.

The only real change to the group over the years, other than individual expansion due to fine dining was that advancing years dictated a late start for whatever adventure the day would bring. This day would be no exception. The evening celebrations were not helping their mobility in any way and they were all feeling ill effects from near constant gin swilling and the copiously inhaled medicinal herb which they partook of to aid digestion. The previous evening had been a particularly tough one. What with boozing, smoking, rousing discourse around the meaning of life, transcontinental meditation, Dakota Slim's failed attempt at other worldly tourism plus the subsequent floor washing debacle had culminated in all of them being slightly subdued that sunny morn.

The Driver wisely decided collapsing on a beach within the confines of Kona would help revive flagging fortunes and at the same time allow time for rational discussions on where and how the search should continue. When he mentioned to his still vain companions that their obvious declining vigour could be disguised by pretending to be on a snorkeling expedition the deal was sealed. Harri reluctantly decided he would remain part of the brotherhood by once again undertaking that dangerous sport. This even as the thought tightened his colon to the size of a mighty oak's acorn.

Assuming no casualties at the beach they would later undertake another reconnoiter of Kona. There were no real expectations other than White Rhino needing to obtain a small gratuity for she who must be obeyed. This was required to offset the ludicrously expensive stringed instrument he had earlier bought from the one armed man. Even at this late stage of life he still believed he could offset foolish spending habits by purchasing baubles for the other half. Considering he'd taken advice around the purchase and the playing of an *authentic Hawaiian ukulele, hand-made in Malaysia* from a one armed man it was clear his thought processes were suspect.

There was also the issue of the busted mirror on the truck. The Driver never had problems in finding vehicles when he needed them and he seldom worried about leaving them wherever when he was finished with them. As a result he saw little need in dealing with this particular issue and it was a testament to his good nature that he let the others do as they pleased. Or perhaps he'd just had a belly full of their inane focus on things that made little difference to his enjoyment of life.

A trip to the local Toyota dealership was to be arranged while Crazy Dave and White Rhino once again decided to recheck the prices of equipment at the downtown dive shop. Those two had never subscribed to the get the hell in and get the hell out style of shopping that the other's lived by. Thanks to the electronic age the pair each had sufficient devices to hand with which to check prices worldwide to ensure they didn't overpay by even a penny on any purchase. Usually, and unhappily as we have seen this constant verifying of prices generally culminated in anything ever being purchased. There was also a downside to travelling about looking through numerous shops, it tended to use up readies and cash holdings were becoming a problem for half the troop.

So plans of a most rudimentary nature were firmed up as well as they could and the group congratulated themselves on being out the door by 1:00p.m. They were headed for a dip in the refreshing waters of the lovely Pacific right in the centre of Kona at Kahaluu Beach Park. The park was quite small and the sand was quite sharp and hot underfoot. There were already a goodly number of people about enjoying the beach but the guys still found an unattended picnic table beneath a swaying palm to which they staked a claim. Shelter was a requirement as Harri had concerns of surveillance from Sky Lab, that and nearly sixty years of sunshine had beat hell out of his hide.

When they had first arrived at the park Crazy Dave noticed what looked like a bombed out church across the road and being a fervent Catholic of the Roman persuasion ambled across to discern an explanation. The Driver privately having concerns that he might have reached the limits of his tolerance for the others quickly pretended to fall asleep on the sand. As for the rest, they felt that they'd come for a swim and so swim they would. There were numbers of the fairer sex soaking up rays on the boy's walk to the water's edge so our heroes tried to suck it up on the meander to the sea. Tried, you can't make a silk purse out of a sow's ear. Over the course of that afternoon all the adventurers would eventually enter the surf. There was even another turtle in the water and White Rhino was again immediately enraptured.

After a couple of hours of sun and surf sustenance seemed to in order but as mentioned funds were getting low. The Driver, while just about fed up with the group's constant infantile antics, was compassionate around the cash flow limitations placed upon his Canadian friends by the worthless loonie. As always he had a plan and if the boys were willing to put up with no floor and no walls then he knew just the cutrate joint. It seems he'd dined there a few weeks back and had inexplicably lost his shoes. Where the writer comes from one only removes ones shoes for one reason and that one reason isn't to have a beer and a sandwich. Interesting as a review might be we will go no further down this road.

The place turned out to be just what the doctor ordered for a late afternoon nosh and glass or two of the landlord's finest. Their waitress was a delightful young lady with nicely tanned long legs who was remarkably shapely where the two met up. Shapely enough to make any of the five make a fool of himself. She advised them that the place was hosting a slumming type society event later that evening and would be closing up early. This news devastated Dakota Slim and he was rendered unable to order a meal. The problem was his lifelong belief that he must masticate each mouthful of food twenty-nine times before swallowing. It always took a full four hours for him to properly enjoy a meal which was as annoying as it sounds to any one dining with him. The others did feel badly when their meals came so they tossed scraps in his direction. They ate and drank quickly so they'd have time to dig around in the sand on hands and knees in a generous but futile search for the wayward shoes.

Right after that belly and soul satisfying stop the next order of business was another replenishing of supplies and you should again read gin. They also needed to stop at a Home Hardware to purchase what was needed to make rudimentary repairs to the damaged portal to the other side. They may have been rough and tumble tough guys but each of their mother's had instilled in them that you always leave a place in better condition than you found it. Not-with-standing individual abilities of course.

Home Hardware turned out to be a trial of almost biblical proportions. Just like the mainland they had trouble finding what they needed and locating staff to assist proved impossible. The result was they spent way more time in the artificially chilled atmosphere than any of them liked. The weight was heavy on their shoulders as they exited the giant retail monstrosity and White Rhino and Dakota Slim were showing signs of strain. Both insisted they needed to stretch out before they fell down. It was agreed that they would head up the hill for a rest and off they went.

Then out of nowhere half of the fatigued duo insisted that a further stop was required. Crazy Dave had been quite enamoured with the recent kayaking experience. He now told his friends that upon his return to the Great White North he would purchase a similar model to the one he had been mishandling. His shopping style has already been adequately detailed so it should come as no surprise that in spite of his exhaustion he demanded to be immediately taken to a retailer. He wanted to take pictures of price tags to show shopkeepers back home to better help him extort lower pricing.

After a day of sun, sand, saltwater, beer, greasy food and the mental exhaustion that comes with hours of surreptitious glances at beach bunnies, all their heads were pounding out the never-ending rhythm of Fleetwood Mac's unwarranted 1979 hit, *Tusk*. Nobody had the energy, nor the inclination, to point out the obvious flaw in Crazy Dave's approach. Never the less The Driver promptly careened into a parking lot outside the first recreational equipment shop they came upon. Crazy Dave promptly wandered off into a pet store.

You see in the late 70's he'd given his head a solid whack whilst trying to maneuver himself through the back seat into the mammoth trunk of a momentarily pristine 1966 Pontiac Parisienne. It was somewhere within the majestic mountains of western Canada and he was on a mission to retrieve car keys that Teacher had earlier placed in the trunk for safe keeping. Since that incident his ability to focus was never quite what it once was or should have been.

In exasperation of Crazy Dave wandering off The Driver entered the shop and immediately laid eyes on a two person kayak. Before anyone could say "who wants a gin" it was bought and secured to the roof of the truck in a much more professional manner than that other day's adventure. There was no way this one would be able to escape. When Crazy Dave ambled back half an hour later he had the odd grin on his face he gets whenever he sees even a picture of a dog. He'd completely forgotten about kayaks.

It had been a great day, each of the desperados had happily put up with whatever minor idiosyncrasies any of them might have picked up over a lifetime of self-indulgence. The thing that stuck out in their relationship was that they all cared for and looked out for each other, especially The Driver who was extraordinarily patient and generous. These were not just friends, but brothers, and it showed in everything that happened and everything they did. They had all slipped back to days when they were twenty and had no need of proving anything, teach anything, compete for anything and it was all quite refreshing. Nothing really mattered but friendship. Egos, money, prestige or even family, was unimportant at that point in time. They were as one but didn't yet realize they were closing in on that which they were searching.

Back at the house they ate a fine meal and once again settled in for an evening of fellowship liberally lubricated with the net result of boiling sprits with botanicals. No television, local radio, or papers had been seen for the week. They had no idea of what had or hadn't happened outside of the world that was created on that hillside. It was just five old friends who had fully reconnected the second they'd arrived on the island. They just enjoyed being together. It was just as it had been back in the swirling grey mists of time.

There may have been no radio or TV but there was music. In another of the never ending strokes of luck Dakota Slim had discovered that one of his electronic implements could pick up Sirius radio signals over the house's WiFi. While not all were sure just exactly what either of those things were they all understood that they were able to select a soundtrack to accompany any scene or potential debacle. With speakers in all the rooms as well as on the patio a constant diet of tunes from the 60's and 70's were played at sometime earsplitting volume. The music reminded them of what they had once been and helped transport them back to those happy days.

The night progressed as all others had. The five indulged in a mind bending blend of gin, beer, smoke, rum, margaritas and interestingly so late in the week, the introduction of pina coladas.

CHAPTER 10

The last day, and it would prove a relief. The week had wrecked havoc on them all and it was thought, or perhaps even somewhere verbalized, that two weeks would have killed them. Like every morning they chowed down on an incredibly cholesterol heavy, though hearty breakfast washed down with copious amounts of coffee in the vain hope that it would help clear their heads.

Immediately after breakfast The Driver's phone rang bringing good news from his daughter. She'd passed the bar exam which meant The Driver would never again need a shady solicitor to put together a shady deal with a shady guy like Shady Norm. He strut around the patio like a peacock, or more aptly, a feral chicken for half an hour and his friends joyfully shared in his happiness.

By now the hideout was looking a bit rough and at the true owners' next visit it would be obvious that unwelcomed pests had been about. Once again taking control of domestic duties Dakota Slim jumped to it and assigned chores which were attacked with gusto in an effort to right all wrongs and correct all mishaps. When they had done it was hard to tell if they'd succeeded but they did try. After a well needed breather from the exertions, plans were put in place for a last wander in town before an early afternoon tea party, followed by one more dip in the sea and one last pizza at the Kona Brewery restaurant. That morning over a last locally grown coffee The Driver announced he was crossing the Rubicon with Shady Norm. Over the course of the week each of the boys had offered up enough unsolicited opinions on Shady Norm's proposed deal to float a battleship. The Driver's head had been kept constantly spinning with an unrelenting tidal wave of *expert* opinions. Hopefully the well intention jabbering did provide a modicum of help towards decision making.

Once the dishes were washed and dried they jumped into the now decidedly worse for wear Toyota and headed uncharacteristically slowly down the hill, a somber mood clearly prevailed. It took a brisk walkabout the town with White Rhino picking some punter's pocket as a lark and a couple of beers at a seaside bar before everyone was back in the spirit of camaraderie that had kept them as one for the past week.

The five intrepid ones had been invited to afternoon tea by the indomitable Shady Norm and The Driver was inclined to take the opportunity to seal the deal. Everything was going well at the soiree until they were introduced to a newly hired diver. When he announced he hailed from Alaska alarm bells immediately went off and red flags went up inside their anesthetized brains. Another person met from elsewhere and from Alaska yet, that land of rough and tumble where men were known to do anything for money! Suddenly nerves got the best of The Driver and he told the boys *"today is not the day to make such a big decision"*. The entire Tanqueray Crew was secretly relieved. The event though did provide the boys with one last opportunity of gazing at pretty girls. They also filled their gobs with free sushi and supped tea from china cups with the proper etiquette of pinkies pointing heavenward or upward dependant on belief. To bolster The Driver's profile they tried hard to appear to be part of some sort of big shot consortium he had brought in from the mainland. Most observers would have opined they failed miserably, but all had fun trying.

When it was time to go, and after prying White Rhino off a blond cutie they headed for remote Mahai'ula Beach. The beach was accessed by a long drive through a five hundred year old lava flow of black rock that could cut bare feet to ribbons. The road had been run through where it had been the easiest so it swung wildly to the left and right, up over ridges and deep down into gullies. A normal driver would have just poked along to prevent damage to the vehicle but not The Driver. The Toyota moved about like a basketball in the hands of Magic Johnson resulting in the boys in the back bouncing off each other like a super-ball in a concrete culvert.

The truck was ultimately parked in a makeshift spot that was little more than a level spot on the lava and the boys legged it down a tortuous path to the beach. It was frightfully hot but the beach was akin to an oasis within the centre of the shifting sands of the Sahara. An oasis of a small white sand beach fringed with swaying palm trees set amongst a black Mars like landscape. The lava flow frozen in time had somehow magically been diverted around this pristine section of paradise. Americans don't seem to want to walk much anymore so the difficulty in access and the heat meant that the beach was nearly deserted and the boys swam and wandered about enjoying the solitude. They had feelings akin to playing hooky from school by escaping out an unguarded classroom window. Fortuitously no wayward 2x4 fell from above on to someone's head while they did so this time.

It was truly a beautiful spot although quite surreal when they glanced about at the lava on all sides. This would be the last swim in Hawaiian waters for some time for most of them. Incredibly there was another turtle for White Rhino, another stubbed toe for Harri, another snorkel for Crazy Dave and time for The Driver to relax on the sand out in the sun. There was also another opportunity for Dakota Slim to take much longer than reasonably necessary to change in and out of his trunks.

It was on this beach on that final day that Crazy Dave gave voice to the thought that each had considered privately whilst enjoying the therapeutic benefits of pool, hot tub and blue Pacific that week. While glancing about at the beat up and woefully out of shape carcasses of his four friends he sadly lamented *"when did we all grow teats"*.

Unhappily the solitude was regularly ruined by a large US government spy plane crisscrossing the area searching for something or someone. The boys were pretty sure what they were looking for and since everyone was hungry a return to The Driver's favourite restaurant seemed in order. This time the crowds were not as large and they were shown to a table almost at once. Maybe the manager with the wonky eyes had left instructions. This last supper, as with the more famous one was tinged with sadness.

They had been on edge since the spy plane earlier that afternoon and their reinvigorated vigilance at dinner paid off in spades. The Driver and Harri spotted the ringer immediately as they sat down. A long leggy blond in a slinky green sheath that made her delightful backside move about like two cats wrasslin' in a silk sack sashayed into the place. Suddenly traffic within the joint stopped dead as did all conversation. It was all the boys could do to not brush up against her to determine where she had concealed her gat. Even after some minutes of intense viewing and clandestine picture taking they were unable to suss out its hiding place, and she had been seated at the next table. Strangely White Rhino didn't seem to notice the broad which was quite troubling to his pals.

After dinner they drove back to the house in a somber mood to shower off the Hawaiian sand and pack their bags. The trip was coming to its inevitable end and while sitting about in quiet reflection they recognized the dead soldiers of the week. What had started out being utilized for purely medicinal purposes had degraded into something much more darkly sinister. Multiple gallons of gin, countless cases of beer and numerous quarts of various other alcoholic libations had been disposed of without malice aforethought. Not to mention the heaping handfuls of the modern equivalent to Maui Wowie that had gone up in smoke to satisfy their constant nonstop self-indulgence in aiding their digestive systems.

It was now all over and they would need to be on the way to the airport by a quarter to ten that night. The last margarita for the road seemed somewhat stronger than normal.

CHAPTER 11

The Driver hurried them out to the truck with what seemed like unseemly haste. He was given the benefit of the doubt due to common knowledge of his well known respect for authority. It had always been his position that if the Man wanted one at the airport a certain number of hours before a flight, then that was rightly what one should do. The good-byes at the airport were heartfelt and there was true sadness in their farewell embraces. They all wished and hoped that they would be able to meet again as a group sometime and each insisted they would try. Each knew in their hearts that it might not be as simple the next time, Crazy Dave wiped away a tear. The boys were left standing on the curb as The Driver motored off into the night to return the Toyota to where it belonged. When they spun round on their heels they found the check-in counter seemed to abut the public sidewalk and there were five people in official looking authoritative garb standing about waiting to assist them on their way home.

The Kona airport was an odd structure as airports go, especially in these days of constant security that can be both reassuring and off-putting by its intrusive nature. First up the building had little in the way of walls and consisted mostly of posts supporting a thatch-like roof. Once the pleasant old fashioned style check-in was accomplished the boys were looking to deposit their bags somewhere and the more aggressive amongst them asked *"where do we deposit out bags?"* The reply stopped them cold. *"Down the sidewalk to the end of the building, turn left and mosey along for a bit, you can't miss it, and by the way the security gate is there as well"* one of the staff responded quite pleasantly. This seemed odd as they were still standing outside. Never-the-less having been well trained since birth they did as they were told. White Rhino was starting to sweat. In spite of tough talk and a false bravado about what he was bringing home there was some minor quibble at the back of his head. He wondered if his little secreted parcel might be just illegal enough to find him bunking down with a hundred and fifty kilogram Samoan named Bubba for a couple of years.

They all passed through security with no difficulty in spite of Dakota Slim once again feeling compelled to crack wise. His venom was aimed at an overweight ethnic minority female who was simultaneously trying to drag her screaming child and a meter wide stroller through a half meter wide security gate. Once on the other side the four travelers reconnoitered for obvious threats, and when none were located they congregated just outside their loading gate. Then in what may have been a combination of tiredness, lack of sense of humour, or just ill temper Harri made some smart retort that he knew intuitively had hurt his old friend Dakota Slim. Why he couldn't intuitively know something before he opened his mouth had always been his problem. The better man bit his tongue and chose to wander off for awhile and check emails. This irresponsible irritation had passed by time they were called for the airplane.

Immediately upon boarding Crazy Dave decided to sit in front of the rest to better monitor the situation and as always watch their backs, figuratively. He couldn't literally watch their back from in front now could he? He was soon firmly ensconced in 8D and wouldn't move for the duration. Harri was in 13F, the emergency exit row for the door to the wing. Once again the powers that be felt he was the right man for the job. White Rhino was seated in a row of three at the window in 14A. His seat mates were a married couple who would have been ill served in a row of six. Dakota Slim was in 17C and was actually literally watching their backs.

As passengers were settling in Harri glanced back and saw White Rhino being sucked into the woman's, or it might have been her husband's massive bosom as seat belts were being fastened. Then as if on signal the married pair simultaneously folded their arms onto their respective chests just beneath their respective multiple chins and White Rhino disappeared from sight. This last view of his friend and the accompanying look of terror on his face caused tears to well up in Harri's eyes and stream down his cheeks. He rushed forward to their security expert but was unable to verbalize the problem. The tears were accompanied by a shortage of air and he couldn't seem to get his breath past the convulsions.

Harri was needlessly concerned. White Rhino having always been one to take the bull by the horns had espied a vacant seat at 13D and pounced on the opportunity. He later related to his dumbfounded friends how he had quickly exhaled his breath while simultaneously releasing his seat belt. This caused a massive release in pressure that launched him across the aisle and into the vacant seat.

They were all pretty tired and each in his way tried to get some rest. Crazy Dave fell sound asleep and wouldn't recall the take off. Dakota Slim had once again successfully played his gastric discomfort card so had two vacant seats beside him on which he stretched out. After the recent near death experience in 14A followed closely by the troubling instructions of the stewardess around emergency procedures White Rhino found he was too wound up to rest. He chose to read another from his seemingly endless supply of science magazines while Harri dozed fitfully on and off during the five hour flight.

Upon arrival at Vancouver International Airport the foursome was strangely alert. They always tried to remain alert since the day many years back when they had seen a notice carved on the beverage-room's washroom wall in The St. Vital Hotel. The notice had boldly proclaimed *be alert, for Canada needs lerts,* they'd taken it to heart.

There was something off-putting in the welcoming fragrant Canadian air that was almost tangible. What they had sensed and feared since leaving a week earlier was now painfully clear. They had been under surveillance and it became obvious that instant. It had all been a sham: the woman at the Winnipeg Airport in the MasterCard kiosk zeroing in on White Rhino, the young lady getting airsick next to Crazy Dave on the first flight, Leo and his Kiwi friend just happening to run into Dakota Slim in the Vancouver departure lounge, the helicopter circling the first dive site, the woman in green eyeballing Harri till he stubbed his toe on the path, the spy plane continually flying over the deserted beach, all the people from Alaska and Shady Norm being so insistent on picking up The Driver at the airport. How could they have missed it all when they had all sensed something? All their precautions had been for naught.

There at the Vancouver Airport in the crowds of milling people Crazy Dave felt a chill go up his abnormally curved spine. It was almost like that frigid first blast of cold air as one stepped outside the house on a Winnipeg January morning, almost, but not exactly.

There in that crowd of travelers Crazy Dave caught a brief yet clear view of that accursed robotic genius Chicken McKay and his villainous henchman Evil Ivol. The latter and The Driver had been good friends all through public school. He had always been an even tempered and good natured fellow but one day had unexpectedly snapped after hearing the phrase -*does Ivol ball*- just once too often. Evil Ivol had disappeared physically off the face of the earth some forty years past, though it had been rumoured in dark corners that he was the muscle for Chicken McKay. His presence was still occasionally felt by the boys as a sudden pervasive sense of doom along with a simultaneous chill in the air.

Chicken McKay and Crazy Dave had been associates in a number of understandings in their high school years. Understandings that while excellent money making endeavours were considered by the authorities to be too much of a detriment to society as whole to be allowed to continue. Later Crazy Dave had sponsored Chicken McKay into the Tanqueray Crew but before too much time passed it was obvious that he was just too far off the wall to be part of the group. He was let down as nicely as possible during a meeting at the Paddlewheel Restaurant over a fine meal of that establishment's excellent roast beef dinner with all the trimmings. The Tanqueray Crew thought the fairness in which it was handled was sufficient to allow all involved to move on. It turned out it hadn't been for one of them.

Chicken McKay had always been a cagey campaigner and spent his life working where he had easy access to anyone on earth he wished to monitor or control. He had become a tax accountant for Revenue Canada. His passion though had always been blending mind control with animal robotics. Each of the boys realized at the same moment that *my little red headed friend Helmut* had not been an ordinary feral chicken. Chicken McKay had perfected his life's work.

Minutes later after the shock wore off their razor sharp instincts kicked in and the boys immediately became attuned to the danger. Those indescribable attributes that had kept them alive for decades were suddenly at the fore and they knew instinctively that they needed a diversion to affect an escape. Any plans of a final meal together or even a quick caper in Chilliwack were immediately shelved. Crazy Dave as elder of the group had always been the mentor and protector of his younger compatriots and true to form immediately insisted that they blow town immediately. Dakota Slim moved first and ran gazelle like through the terminal and grabbed a cab for the ferry. It was actually more like the spirited airport run once made by OJ but that comparison might have been insensitive.

The other three were not so lucky, their flight was not scheduled to depart for three hours. With little forethought and no regard whatsoever for the impact on his high yield interest rate savings account

Crazy Dave quickly pulled a few hundred from his secret hiding place and thrust them into their hands hoarsely whispering "*take an earlier flight and leave Chicken McKay and that goon Evil Ivol to me, oh, and fly through Edmonton as I've heard the Chili's Restaurant in the terminal is to die for*". Then he picked up the large bag containing the tools of his trade and slipped into the throng as seamlessly as a cat slips into a bathtub of water. He had that look in his eye the others knew so well. Things that had to be done were going to be done and things were going to go badly for someone. Once safely aboard the flight home White Rhino and Harri would later comment that if he had money squirreled away why had he spent the last day and a half borrowing money from them?

Leaving Crazy Dave to his self-appointed task the duo rushed as told to get the flight through Edmonton. It was true that Crazy Dave had only made a recommendation but a life time of association with *Turkey Legs* and his temper left the two with no alternative. They would do as they had been instructed including dining at Chili's. The meal wouldn't turn out that good but they would never tell him so.

The flights were uneventful and both were so mentally and physically exhausted from the stress at the airport they dozed off and on for most of the trip. Somewhere over Saskatchewan the captain pointed out a 747 flying beneath them that was quite clear to see. Moments later there was another off to the right. Neither of our travelers had ever seen airplanes that close on other flights, never mind two. They didn't get out much and were very easily impressed.

CHAPTER 12

All made it home alive with stories to tell.

The Driver had hung about Hawaii for an extra day to recover, clean up and gather what remained of his wits. What a *f-x-x-x-i-n-g* week he mused under his breath countless time. The highlight for him had been on the boat when in childlike wonder Harri and White Rhino went reef chumming with half digested fish and cheese burgers. The memory would doubtless bring him to his knees in laughter for years to come.

When he went to start packing for his return journey he discovered some Oregon herb and an oddly erotic shaped smoking device. He'd inadvertently left them in his bag on a previous mission to his bolt-hole in Portland Oregon, actually Vancouver Washington but that is splitting hairs. He had forgotten all about them being in the bag when he had left for the island and had evidently carried the contraband through security in Portland while en-route to Hawaii. The items had either not been detected or was not considered a big deal by the powers that be, or maybe nobody wanted to mess with him. Still, the thought of what might have happened brought a tightness to his chest and a shortness of breath that was worrying for a moment or two.

On the flight back while in a moment of whimsy he recalled that on the day of the reception at Shady Norm's establishment he could not locate a belt. Not that he needed a belt as he'd maintained the same slim physique; some would say almost ballerina like figure since he'd been twenty. Anyway, on the way to Shady Norm's that afternoon he had found a piece of black plastic strapping laying on the side of the road. Inventive and resourceful person that he'd always been he quickly and masterfully fashioned it into a belt. In addition to inventive and resourceful he had always been generous to a fault and at the same time was also very concerned with environmental issues. Once he had no further use of the homemade item he could just not bring himself to discard of it. He'd placed it in Crazy Dave's bag, who wouldn't discover his friend's generosity until his return home. Having been brought up by a gentle woman, Crazy Dave immediately damned the long distance expense and called The Driver to thank him for the thoughtful gift. He's been wearing the belt in honour of his old friend ever since.

When immediately back in the good old US of A, The Driver was unexpectedly approached to invest his modest resources in a new venture that, in his wildest dreams, suggested that he could yet strike it rich. His accidental discovery a few months back that the mere addition of sugar to a little known toxic substance that, in addition to its mind altering qualities when ingested by humans, had the ability to prevent udder infections in bovines seemed to have unlimited retail possibilities. Who knew where it could end? What he did know was that the Crew had been unaware they'd been unwitting guinea pigs of the substance a few times over the past week and it did trouble him somewhat. The Driver decided then and there he would deal with his conscience when the bucks started to roll in.

Dakota Slim reported no problems with any transportation schedule other than the Max refusing to pick him up at the ferry terminal. He'd been forced to walk home the twelve miles as he hadn't a penny in his TK's, other than a $100 bill which he refused to break. Fortunately pension day was only a half week off.

Harri was staggered by all he'd done and seen. He was more than ever thankful that he had worked at staying in contact with his old friends for all those years. When he related some of the more mundane tales to others he was always struck by the invariable comment that staying so close to the same bunch for all those years was remarkable and unusual. He had to agree.

White Rhino's story was best, although somewhat incoherent. It was faxed to the rest of the Crew some weeks after the uproar died down.

"Relive the past. It was something we could not do when we were eighteen and couldn't do in-between then and now. Just pick up and go. It felt recklessly delicious to just book a trip thousands of kilometers away at the drop of a hat. It felt deserving to be able to just spend money without a second thought. It felt surreal to be in a paradise of luxury unknown to most of the world while being grey and wrinkled but feeling young. There was always a silent feeling of limitations hanging in the air; age, money, wives, morals, each others foibles and strengths. It turned out to be a renewal of old bonds and finding humour in long past mistakes and stupidity. We captured a moment that I'm sad to say we will never be able to recreate but will always wish we could and will continue to try. I reel with emotion just below the surface when I drift through the memories of beaches, sand, majestic views, oxygen deprivation, sunsets, gin, smoke and so much more that words can't paint. It's the best of life and we should live it every day."

As a group they realized over the weeks to follow that they hadn't found what they had been looking for. They hadn't found it because it hadn't been lost. It had been inadvertently hidden away behind everything that had gone on since the 70's. It was as though forty years of life had been lifted from their shoulders for a week. They were teenagers again bouncing around St. Vital trying to scrape up $2.50 for gas so they could enjoy themselves. The individual flotsam that had been generated over decades of living had hidden and glossed over who they really were and what they'd always been.

That was why the past week seemed so surreal, nothing had changed. They were just what they'd always been.

Friends ....

THE END

Carl H. Harrison was born in Hull, Yorkshire, England, but grew up and currently resides in Winnipeg, Manitoba, Canada. He attended the University of Manitoba before starting a career with a major Canadian bank.

Harrison retired early and spent his days traveling. He recounts his travels in the Harri's on Tour series, a collection of lighthearted travel books.

White Rhino and the Tanqueray Crew is his first work of fiction.

Made in the USA
Charleston, SC
29 December 2015